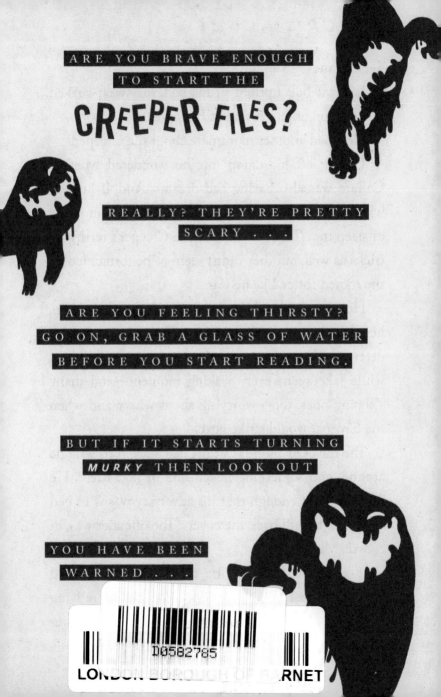

ARE YOU BRAVE ENOUGH
TO START THE
CREEPER FILES?

REALLY? THEY'RE PRETTY
SCARY . . .

ARE YOU FEELING THIRSTY?
GO ON, GRAB A GLASS OF WATER
BEFORE YOU START READING.

BUT IF IT STARTS TURNING
MURKY THEN LOOK OUT

YOU HAVE BEEN
WARNED . . .

'Get off me!'

Jake sat bolt upright in his bed, his sweat-soaked T-shirt clinging to his body. He sighed.

He'd had another nightmare about the Creeper.

Pulling off his damp top, he wondered whether Callum was also having bad dreams. And, if he was, why weren't Liam and Sarah complaining about a lack of sleep too? They'd witnessed the Creeper's terrifying tricks as well, but they didn't seem to be tormented by the rooted rotter, like he was.

However it was they were managing to keep calm, he wished they could teach him. They appeared to be determined to relax and enjoy the summer holidays, while Jake spent every waking moment—and many sleeping ones, too—worrying about where and when the Creeper would strike next.

The duvet at the foot of his bed started to wriggle around, and something licked one of Jake's feet. He felt confident enough that his adversary wasn't in bed with him to pull back the covers. The offender was, of course, Max.

'I knew you wouldn't be too far away,' chuckled Jake. He gave the dog a pat on the head before lying back down. But Max had other plans. He leapt over

Jake's legs, trotted across the room, and rested a paw up against the door.

'You want to go out now?' groaned Jake, checking the time on his phone.

2.12 a.m.

Max gave a quiet *snuff* and padded back to the bed to lick his hand.

'Alright,' said Jake, wiping the slobber off on his pyjamas. He grabbed a dry T-shirt and pulled it on as he opened the bedroom door.

The pair made their way downstairs and into the darkened kitchen, where a sudden flash of green light made Jake stop suddenly. The eerie light lit up the entire wall for a second, then disappeared.

Then it was back. And gone again. Back. And gone again.

Could it be that the Creeper was somehow—

No, it was the clock on the microwave, flashing 12:00 on its black face. Jake allowed himself to breathe again as he remembered the short power cut they'd had earlier that evening. The clock just needed resetting.

Telling himself off for being so jittery, Jake unlocked the back door and pulled it open so that Max could nip out and take care of his business—only to find the Creeper stood waiting on their doorstep!

OXFORD
UNIVERSITY PRESS

Great Clarendon Street, Oxford OX2 6DP

Oxford University Press is a department of the University of Oxford.
It furthers the University's objective of excellence in research, scholarship,
and education by publishing worldwide. Oxford is a registered trade mark
of Oxford University Press in the UK and in certain other countries

British Library Cataloguing in Publication Data

Data available

ISBN: 978-0-19-274732-7

1 3 5 7 9 10 8 6 4 2

Printed in Great Britain

Paper used in the production of this book is a natural,
recyclable product made from wood grown in sustainable forests.
The manufacturing process conforms to the environmental
regulations of the country of origin.

HACKER MURPHY'S

CREEPER
FILES

TERROR
FROM THE TAPS

OXFORD
UNIVERSITY PRESS

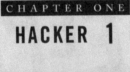

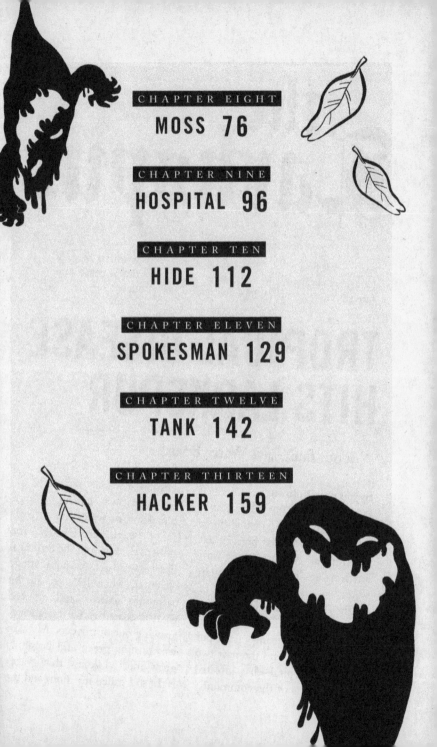

the Larkspur

TROPICAL DISEASE HITS LARKSPUR

Not our fault, says Water Board

By our man in town,
HACKER MURPHY

Residents of Larkspur have been hit by what has been called a "tropical" disease and "not anything at all to do with the tap water."

The illness—which has seen one youngster, eleven-year-old Callum Ball from Larkspur High School, spend the past two nights in hospital—has affected different parts of the community in different ways.

'I was just having a nice cold drink of water before bed,' Callum explained through the rubber curtain of the tropical diseases ward of Larkspur Cottage Hospital, 'when I looked in the bathroom mirror and noticed what appeared to be tiny carrots growing out of my ears. My skin was turning green and began to grow moss. I knew that wasn't right so I called my mum and she

brought me to the hospital.'

Mr Melvyn Mulwray, spokesman for Larkspur Water Board, was quick to contradict the boy however. 'The Ball boy may indeed have presented with the slightest emerald glow—quite becoming and healthy-looking in fact—but who's to say just how long those carrots have been sprouting from his ears? They could have been there for months. This is very unlikely to have been anything to do with him drinking our fresh, untainted water supply.'

I offered Mr Mulwray the chance to drink a glass of tap water, but he declined. 'I bought a bottle of spring water in the hospital shop,' he explained. 'I don't want to let that, er . . . go off or anything.'

CHAPTER ONE

HACKER

Hello again. I'm really pleased you've come back to read more from my increasing collection of facts and information in The Creeper Files.

You'll already know that the Creeper raised an army of potato-men, the battle against which resulted in Larkspur High School exploding.

There was also the strange case of plants attacking a campsite that some of Larkspur's pupils were attending.

Could it be that this half-man, half-plant monster—named by a trio of young, local residents as the Creeper—has a personal vendetta against children at that school?

It certainly seemed that way when a porter at

the local hospital called this morning to give me a tip-off. I made a note of the phone conversation to add to my files.

'Hello, is that the Larkspur Chronicle?'

'Yes, it is. Hacker Murphy speaking. How can I help?'

'My name's Roberts. I'm a porter at Larkspur Cottage Hospital. I understand you pay for stories . . .'

'We do when I can get my editor to authorize payment, but that's not very often. Why, what do you know?'

(LONG PAUSE)

'Mr Roberts?'

'There's something very funny happening up here . . .'

'Funny? What do you mean, funny?'

'It's a boy. Admitted last night. I wheeled him up to the ward myself.'

'And this boy's not well?'

'I should say so. Not with green, tufty skin.'

'Green, tufty—'

'Like moss, it is. You should come and see for yourself.'

(CLICK)

Of course, I went straight to my editor with the news. This had to be the work of the Creeper! But he wasn't buying my argument, nor was he buying this porter's info. I rifled through my desk drawers and managed to scrape together £13.50. Probably not the reward Mr Roberts was expecting, but it was all I could manage.

It didn't matter anyway. What mattered was I was hot on the Creeper's tail once more . . .

CHAPTER TWO

HUNTED

Jake felt his lungs burn with every breath as he slid across the muddy pathway. He grabbed a low-hanging branch, ducked beneath it and took off across a small clearing in the woodland. The long grass swished against the lower parts of his legs as he ran, a temporary respite from the sharp bushes and tree roots that had almost seemed determined to delay his escape.

There were footsteps echoing behind him. The footsteps of someone giving chase along the path. Footsteps which sounded as though they were made by wooden feet.

And it was too much for Jake to hope that he was being pursued by a resident of the Netherlands wearing a pair of traditionally carved clogs.

He risked a glance over his shoulder and, through the dark, forbidding forest, he could just make out a tall, thin shape dodging easily between the trees.

If he squinted, it appeared that the top of the figure had a gaping mouth, brown mottled skin, and piercing green eyes which were fixed directly on him.

The monster's next victim.

Suddenly, Jake's foot caught on a root rising up from the ground. He glanced down at the root that had tripped him, but it had vanished. Now there was nothing but mud.

The creature was up to his tricks again.

Jake ran on, twigs and low-hanging branches whipping across his face.

He was certain he could feel the searing hot breath of the beast on the back of his neck as it drew closer and closer, waiting for the chance to attack.

This time, the Creeper was going to get him.

They both knew it.

He knows this place, Jake thought to himself. *This is his territory. He's probably chasing me towards the deepest, darkest area of the forest right now, so there won't be any witnesses to the attack.*

The thought spurred Jake into action, and he darted sideways off the path, towards a dense group of trees. *Come on then, Fungus Face!* he thought. *If I'm going down, then you'll have to catch me first*.

There was a CRACK!, like the sound of a whip, and a long tendril struck the trunk of the tree nearest to Jake, tearing away the bark and revealing the pale, wet wood beneath.

Jake swallowed hard as he realized that was pretty much what would happen to his flesh if the Creeper managed to land one of those tendrils directly on—

CRACK!

Another thick length of vine exploded through the air beside Jake's face, causing his right ear to ring loudly and painfully.

CRACK!

This time the tendril connected, wrapping itself tightly around the boy's bare ankle and tugging him backwards. Jake crashed to the muddy ground with an OOF! as the wind was knocked out of him.

He heard a snarl and flipped himself over on to his back just in time to witness the Creeper bearing down on him, his eyes flashing wildly and jaw gaping. Inside his mouth were several rows of sharp, splinter-like teeth. They gnashed together as the beast made another sound. A different sound, like someone sawing through the rotten branches of a diseased tree.

The Creeper was laughing at him!

Another tendril snaked up Jake's free leg, lashing itself to a thick root that had risen from the mud beside him. Two more of these vines were pinning him down in the dirt by his shoulders.

Jake screwed his hands into fists, but he knew it was a useless gesture. The Creeper's long, wooden arms were almost double the length of his own. His captor would be able to crush the life from his body while Jake lashed out at the air between them in vain.

There was only one thing left he could try . . .

'Please!' he begged. 'I know the plant hasn't taken over completely. I know there's still some human inside you. I'm talking directly to that human now. Don't hurt me!'

But Jake could only watch as the Creeper's long, wooden fingers rolled inwards to form a thick fist. The beast grinned as he raised his hand high in the air, and brought it down—

7

'AARGH!'

Jake sat bolt upright in bed, still screaming.

It had all been a nightmare. Another nightmare.

Or had it? His pyjamas were soaking wet, as though he had been rolling around in the mud—or, more likely, because he'd been sweating under his bed clothes.

Although there was a thick tendril beneath the duvet, wrapped round his leg . . . Cautiously, Jake reached down towards it with his hand. The vine wasn't cold and slimy, as he'd imagined it would be. Instead, it was warm and covered with thick fur.

It moved beneath his hand, patting repeatedly against his thigh. If the Creeper was trying to injure him, he wasn't doing a very good job. Still, Jake knew he had to free himself from the monster's grip. Steeling himself, he whipped back the bedcovers . . .

. . . to reveal that it wasn't a tendril wrapped around his leg after all—it was a dog's tail.

And it was attached to the rest of the family pet who had, somehow, managed to get into Jake's bed without waking him.

'Oh so you've decided to show up, have you?' Jake muttered shakily to Max. 'Where were you when I needed saving from the Creeper?'

RRFF! grunted Max in reply, planting a slobbery lick on the boy's cheek.

Jake scratched the pooch behind the ear. 'Yep, that's exactly the big scary hound I could have done with a few minutes ago.'

A soft knock on the bedroom door made him jump. Man, he was on edge tonight.

'Jake, are you OK?' It was Mum's voice. 'You were shouting again.'

'Yeah, sorry if I woke you up,' Jake called back, swinging his legs off the bed and switching on the lamp. 'I just had a bad dream. I'm fine, don't worry.'

Jake checked the time as he pulled off his sweat-soaked T-shirt and grabbed a fresh pair of pyjamas from the chest of drawers.

3.27 a.m.

He sighed heavily. This was the third night this week he'd been woken by a Creeper nightmare. It was a good job the summer holidays had started or he'd be sleepwalking his way through school.

Deciding to leave the lamp on for a while, Jake slumped back against the pillow. 'Yuck!' he moaned.

'Soaking wet!'

He was turning the pillow over when he noticed that Max was standing at the bedroom door, looking expectantly back at him.

'Oh, what now?' Jake grumbled. 'You can't want to go out at this time of night!'

Max gave an almost inaudible whimper.

'Alright,' said Jake, climbing back out of bed and opening the door. 'But you'd better learn to use the bathroom soon, or you'll be holding it in all night.'

Not wanting to disturb his parents any further, Jake made his way downstairs by the moonlight streaming in through the windows. It wasn't quite a full moon tonight, but there was enough light to cast an eerie glow around the interior of the house.

Reaching the back door, Jake turned the key and allowed Max to bound outside. Immediately, the dog became determined to find exactly the right spot by sniffing what appeared to be every square centimetre of the garden.

Jake shivered against the stiff breeze, wishing he'd grabbed his dressing gown on the way down. The droplets of sweat still clinging to the back of his hair felt like they were starting to freeze.

'Hurry up, Max!' he hissed out into the dead night air. The snuffling pooch was now little more than another silhouette somewhere in the darkness.

The trees at the far end of the garden rustled in the wind, and it was all Jake could do not to imagine the Creeper hiding out there somewhere, watching his every move, ready to pounce when the time was right. And that wasn't too much of a stretch for the imagination.

Ever since he and his twin friends Liam and Sarah had first encountered the half-man, half-plant monster, it seemed to have carved a particular hatred for the trio in its herbivore heart. Perhaps it was because they were the first people to stand up to the Creeper and realize his true identity? Not, as they first thought, their new health-obsessed headteacher, Mr Campion. Or their temporarily missing botany teacher, Professor Bloom.

It was the school's lab assistant—Woody Hemlock—who had transformed into the photosynthesizing freak that was now terrorizing the town. Not that anyone seemed to believe them about it whenever they tried to report the problem. Even after Woody had raised an entire army of misshapen potato-men to attack them, blowing up the school in the process.

The Creeper had found a way to shape-shift into one of the two group leaders at their recent school camp, in an attempt to control the forest for his own putrid purposes.

On both occasions, things could have been a lot worse for the residents of Larkspur if it wasn't for the bravery and quick thinking of Jake, Liam, and Sarah.

But it wasn't over yet. The Creeper was still out there somewhere.

Waiting. Watching. Eager for another chance to attack, and build a world of flourishing flora, reversing the harm humans had done to the planet.

Jake felt a shiver run down his spine, although he wasn't convinced it was down to the cold night air.

'Come on, Max!' he called in a loud whisper. 'You must have finished by now!'

Right on cue, the dog trotted up the garden and in through the back door, as if he didn't have a care in the world.

'I don't suppose you do have any cares really, do you, boy?' Jake asked him as he locked the door and the pair made for the stairs. 'You'll be snoring away again in no time, whereas I doubt that I'll get to sleep again for the rest of the night!'

CHAPTER THREE

SPOTTED

'Wake up, sleepyhead!'

Jake started as a tartan rucksack landed on the grass beside his head. 'Huh?'

Sarah spread out a large towel and settled down beside her drowsy friend. 'I thought you were coming down to watch the swimming contest?'

Jake blinked against the bright sunlight, trying to gather his bearings. He was lying on a slope at the end of the local open-air swimming pool, Larkspur Lido. Around them were scores of other people—either splashing about in the water or just lounging in the early summer sun.

'Yeah,' he croaked. 'Of course.'

'But you decided you'd rather sleep through it,

13

instead?'

'I had a bad night last night,' said Jake, rubbing his eyes.

Sarah looked concerned. 'More nightmares?'

Jake nodded. 'I'm shattered.'

'Being chased by the Creeper again?'

'Ssshhh!' urged Jake, glancing round to make sure that no one was listening in. 'You'll have people thinking I've gone crazy.'

Sarah shrugged. 'Everyone we've tried to tell about the Creeper so far already thinks you're crazy.'

'Alright,' sighed Jake. 'You'll have even *more* people thinking I'm crazy.' He paused to look around. 'Where's Liam?'

'Gone to get changed with "the gang",' Sarah replied. 'He's become a real pain since he got involved in this swimming-team nonsense. I think I preferred him when you two used to lounge around all day playing video games.'

'At least this gets him out of the house and exercising,' Jake offered, realizing how scarily like his mum he sounded.

'That's not the problem,' Sarah explained. 'It's when he gets home that he's at his most annoying. He never shuts up about the team, or the pool, or the next contest.'

A smattering of applause rang out as the door to the lido's changing rooms opened and the visiting team jogged out. A mixture of teenage boys and girls, they each wore a matching pale blue tracksuit and swimming cap.

'Ladies and gentlemen,' crackled a tinny voice through the pool's speaker system. 'Please welcome this week's visiting swimmers—the Darracot Dolphins!'

Jake shielded his eyes with his hand and peered at the opposing team down the far end of the pool. 'They don't look too bad.'

'Liam says they've been regional runners-up for the past three years,' said Sarah. 'Could be their turn to win this time.'

Jake grinned and turned his attention back to the changing rooms. 'Not if our lot have got anything to do with it!'

Thin pop music began to echo around the lido as the home team emerged to slightly more applause than had been offered to the visitors.

'Ladies and gentlemen, please go wild for our very own swimming team, still competing hard despite several sudden illnesses, two verrucas, and one stolen swimming costume . . . The Larkspur Lions!'

Liam and his teammates burst through the changing room doors. They were dressed in gold

15

tracksuits and matching caps—although some of the swimmers had abandoned their headgear today to show off their freshly bleached hair.

The team posed while one girl's mum took a photo, then they took an immediate right turn and set off at a confident run around the grassy verge.

'Are they going to do a lap of honour *before* the start of the contest?' said Jake.

Sarah nodded. 'Liam says they're always too tired to do one afterwards, so this is their way of allowing the fans to get a good view of them all.'

'Wow. And have you tried to tell him that Larkspur Lions doesn't exactly work as a name for a swimming team?'

'Yep.'

'In fact, with lions being big cats, they're unlikely to enjoy swimming under any circumstances?'

'Tried that one, too,' Sarah sighed. 'He said they had to be the Lions, or it was the Larkspur Lungfish, which doesn't sound very pleasant.'

'He's got a point,' Jake agreed. 'At least he hasn't given in to this daft idea of dying your hair bleach blond to match the colour of his track—'

Having reached the far end of the swimming pool, Liam whipped off his cap.

'Oh, he has!'

Sarah clamped a hand over her mouth to stifle her laughter. 'He got my mum to do it last night,' she chuckled. 'He's convinced he looks like a rock star.'

Jake stared at his friend, eyes wide. 'He looks more like Max!'

'Don't tell him that!' hissed Sarah. 'He was gutted enough when his self-tanning idea didn't work.'

Jake reached into his bag for a half-empty bottle of fizzy drink. '"Self-tanning idea"?'

Once again, Sarah's hand flew up to cover her mouth. 'He had a bath with a box of forty tea bags!'

PFFFT! Jake spat a mouthful of lukewarm cola over the family sitting in front of them. 'Sorry,' he mumbled. 'Bit of a summer cold!'

Sarah wiped tears from the corners of her eyes. 'He came downstairs looking like my nan's old wardrobe. Took six showers to scrub it all off.'

Jake chuckled as he wiped fizzy pop from his shirt. 'I'm so glad he hasn't managed to talk me into joining the team.'

Sarah raised an eyebrow. 'He's tried to get you involved too, has he?'

'All the time,' said Jake with a nod. 'Especially with people dropping out ill these past few weeks.'

'And you don't fancy it?'

'No, he seems happy with all his new sporty pals. I

17

don't want to step on anyone's toes.'

Sarah gave Jake a gentle punch in the arm. 'Not getting jealous, are you?'

Jake scowled. 'What? Of Teabag Boy and the Doggy Paddlers Club? No chance!' His voice trailed away as he watched Liam tussle with one of the other boys on his team. The other boy made a comment and both of them laughed together.

'No,' Jake said quietly, almost to himself. 'I'm not jealous at all.'

There was a piercing whistle of feedback as the announcer grabbed his microphone and the tannoy system hissed into life. 'Right, we are now ready for the first race of the day, which will be the four by 50 metres freestyle relay. Swimmers, please take your starting positions . . .'

A hush fell over the lido as four members from each team lined up behind their diving podium, taking this last opportunity to bend and stretch out their muscles. Liam was the second swimmer for the Larkspur Lions.

Beside the announcer, a thin figure dressed in a crumpled suit raised a starting pistol to the air. Jake's attention was instantly drawn to the man—not because of his unusual choice of clothing for such a hot day, nor for the realistic-looking weapon he was about to use to start the race.

No, it was the man's eyes that looked eerily familiar. They flashed from behind his wire-framed glasses.

The first two swimmers stepped up on to their respective podiums.

'On your marks . . .' said the announcer. 'Get set . . .'

Suddenly, realization hit home and Jake grabbed Sarah's arm. 'We have to stop the race!'

'What? Why?'

Jake pointed at the figure with the starting pistol. 'That man is the Creeper!'

BANG!

SPLASH!

As soon as the starter fired his gun and the first swimmers hit the water, Jake was up and running.

He dodged past a family unpacking a picnic on to an unfurled blanket, and around a group of toddlers waddling their way towards the children's pool, arms and tummies wrapped in inflatable armbands and rubber rings.

'Wait for me!'

He barely made out Sarah's voice over the cheering of those watching the race as she ran after him.

'Jake!'

But Jake didn't slow his pace. Leaping over a pair of sunbathing girls, he picked up speed along the side of the pool, passing the first swimmer in each team as they raced past—neck and neck—in the opposite direction.

'Jake?' called Liam.

Jake glanced up to see his friend stepping up on to the podium at the far end of the pool. And the Creeper was edging closer to him, the pistol still clutched in his hand.

'It's him!' roared Jake as he ran. 'The Creeper!'

Alarmed, Liam spun on the podium, trying to spot the half-human, half-plant monster. 'What? Where?'

Right beside you, you clown! thought Jake as he jumped over the rail of the metal steps leading down at the edge of the deep end. He landed awkwardly, slipping on the wet tiles around the edge of the pool.

PEEP! The lifeguard blew his whistle loudly. 'No running!' he yelled. 'That means you, too!' he shouted as Sarah sprinted past him.

By the time she rounded the corner to the deep end, all she could do was watch as Jake leapt for the starter, bundling him to the ground. The gun clattered from his hand, allowing Jake to swing out a leg and kick it out of reach.

'Get off me!' cried the man. 'What do you think you're doing?'

'Stopping you from hurting anyone here today!' snarled Jake, sitting down heavily on his captive to stop him from squirming around.

'You're insane!' spat the man.

'Oh, stop with the pretence, Woody!' said Jake. 'Transform back to your normal appearance, and we can leave these people to their swimming.'

Sarah clamped a hand on Jake's shoulder. 'What are you doing?' she demanded, struggling to catch her breath.

'I was just about to ask him the same thing,' said Liam from the podium. He kept one eye on the water as the two first swimmers in each team made their way back towards the start.

'This,' said Jake, 'is the Creeper.'

The man lying beneath Jake blinked. 'I'm the what?'

'Jake,' began Sarah, 'I'm really not sure . . .'

'No!' Jake interrupted. 'I'm tired of being freaked out by this . . . this freak! You know he can change faces to look like a different human whenever he wants.'

'I know,' said Liam. 'He did it with Terry—the youth leader from the school camp we went on.'

'His name wasn't Terry,' Sarah exclaimed. 'It was Dave!'

'It doesn't matter what his name was!' Jake cried. 'He wasn't real, and neither is this guy. It's Woody Hemlock in disguise.' He pinched the man's cheeks and began to pull them in and out. 'Come on Woody, change back and show everyone here what you really look like when you're the Creeper!'

'Did you just call my dad creepy?' demanded one of the girls from the Darracot Dolphins.

'Not creepy,' replied Jake. '*The Creeper*! He's a half-plant . . .' His voice trailed away as he looked up at the girl, the first flickering of uncertainty in his eyes. 'Wait . . . Your dad?'

'Yes,' insisted the girl. 'The person you're sitting on is my dad!'

Jake glanced up to Liam for reassurance, just in time to see his friend dive into the water as the second swimmer for the Lions. No help there, then.

He turned to Sarah instead, but she just shrugged.

'But . . . But, he has green eyes!' Jake flustered.

'So do a lot of people,' said the girl. 'And . . .?'

'They flashed! I saw them flash from across the pool!'

'It's these glasses,' said the man. 'They're always catching the sunlight like that, especially when I'm driving. I need to get some new ones made. I suppose you'll be asking me why the person who started the race had a starting pistol next, will you?'

Jake's stomach flipped as just about every reason he had for pouncing on the man he believed was the Creeper began to evaporate. All, except for one . . .

'Ah!' he cried. 'The suit! Who comes to a swimming

gala in a suit and tie?'

'Someone who has nipped out of the office to give his daughter's team a bit of support in their latest competition, perhaps?' the man suggested. 'Now, if you wouldn't mind . . .'

Nodding apologetically, Jake climbed off the man and helped him to stand.

The starter's clothes were soaking wet.

'I'm . . . I'm sorry,' Jake muttered. 'I mistook you for someone else entirely.'

'Yes,' said the man, straightening his soggy tie. 'It appears that you did.'

Sarah led her friend off to one side. 'What's wrong with you?' she hissed. 'You can't go around knocking people out just because they've got green eyes.'

'It's these nightmares,' Jake moaned, rubbing a hand over his face. 'They're really starting to get to me now. I'm imagining I see that thing everywhere . . .'

Which is when a pair of green eyes flashed at him from beneath the lido's raked seating.

'The Creeper!' he yelled, setting off at a run.

'Not again!' she sighed.

Jake glanced over his shoulder. 'I *mean* it this time!'

Reluctantly, Sarah chased after her friend once again.

CHAPTER FOUR

RECRUIT

Sarah found Jake exploring the murky underside of the lido's seating area. He was using the light from his mobile phone to pick his way through the mounds of damp, slimy debris scattered about.

'I promise you it was him this time,' Jake said, avoiding Sarah's gaze. 'The Creeper.'

Sarah held up her hands. 'What? I didn't say anything.'

'No, but you were about to,' Jake grumbled. 'And Liam would be saying the same thing if he was here instead of playing Aquaman out there.'

'Don't start taking it out on Liam's new hobby,' said Sarah. 'At least he's getting—'

'Look!' hissed Jake. 'He's been here!' He stooped

and ran his fingers through a patch of stringy green leaves at his feet.

Sarah bent to avoid banging her head on the metal struts, and joined him. 'Or . . .' she said slowly, 'some random weeds have managed to grow here in the semi-darkness.'

Jake sniffed at his fingers. 'It's not just that,' he said. 'They feel and smell weird. Like they're coated with something . . .'

He stuck out his tongue and slowly brought his hand towards it.

'No,' began Sarah, 'I wouldn't—'

Jake frowned at her. 'I've dismembered living potato men with my bare hands, and survived an assassination attempt while abseiling. I think I can do a little hands-on detective work without any real danger.'

'OK,' said Sarah, 'But don't say I didn't warn you.'

Licking the tips of his fingers, Jake tried to identify the taste. 'It's sharp,' he said, taking another lick. 'But sour at the same time.'

'Can you compare it to anything?' Sarah asked.

'Ooh, I don't know . . .'

'Is it, for example, like cat pee?'

'Yes,' cried Jake. 'It could be cat pee! Why?'

'Because you do know there's a family of wild cats that live down here? They come out when the lido

25

closes for the night, I've seen them when we collect Liam from training.'

Jake's eyes flicked down to the weeds, and back to his fingers. Then he ran his tongue around the inside of his mouth.

'Oh,' he said, pulling up his T-shirt to wipe his tongue dry. 'Oh yuck!'

'Which is why you should take a step back from this and think for a second,' said Sarah. 'If you go charging in, you're going to make mistakes.'

Jake, however, wasn't listening to her. Instead, he was staring at something over Sarah's shoulder. 'No,' he said, a smile melting into view. 'It's *you* who needs to take a step back—and find out what is through that door behind you.'

Sarah turned to discover a partly open, rusted metal door in the wall.

'When is a door not a door?' quizzed Jake.

'That's an old one, even for you,' said Sarah. 'When it's *ajar*.'

'No,' replied Jake, grinning. 'When it's the entrance to a plant monster's secret hideout! And, also, when it's ajar . . .'

They crept over together. Jake pressed his shoulder against it and pushed. The door swung back with a CRRREAAAKK!, allowing them to step into the dark, musty room beyond. It was filled with clunking, whirring machinery. Every surface was coated with damp, green algae.

'This is it!' hissed Jake. 'The Creeper's lair, and all his equipment.'

'Are you sure?' asked Sarah, but Jake was too excited to listen to any form of reasoning.

'Look, this will be the computer he uses to transform from one human body to another—and here's where he gets his plant powers from . . .' He grabbed an upturned plastic chair and sat down in front of the metal cover to the machinery.

'"Plant powers"?'

'I'm sure there's a technical term, like *sap skills* or *photosynthesis force* or something like that. What I'm saying is, this is the same as the machine Woody had set up in the greenhouse at school.'

Sarah's eyebrows knitted together as she thought back. 'You mean the one that had tree branches and electric cables running in and out of it?'

'That's the one,' confirmed Jake. 'This'll be version 2.0.'

'I really don't want to burst your happy detective bubble,' Sarah said, wiping a layer of algae with her hand. 'But the cover says it's the filtration system for the swimming pool.'

Jake sighed heavily. 'Does it?'

Sarah nodded. 'I'm afraid so.'

Jake jumped up and stared at the wording etched into the metal hatch. 'But, there's all these horrible plant stems sticking out of it.'

'I guess it doesn't get cleaned out very often,' said Sarah. 'Look, I know how important it is for you to find the Creeper—'

'No,' snapped Jake. 'No, you don't. These nightmares are driving me insane, Sarah. He's got inside my head, and—' Suddenly, Jake gasped and grabbed handfuls of his own hair. 'You don't think he's literally inside my head, do you? Is the Creeper concealing himself in my cranium? Am I now the secret hideout for a maniacal plant beast?'

Sarah gently took her friend's hands in her own and lowered them down to his sides. 'OK,' she said slowly. 'So far this afternoon, you've been sounding crazy. But now, you're starting to talk like my brother.'

Jake looked aghast. 'Like Liam? Seriously?'

Sarah nodded.

'Maybe I am taking all this a bit far,' he admitted. 'Perhaps I do need to take my mind off—'

'Excuse me?'

The pair spun to face the door. Standing just inside the room was a ginger-haired boy of around five-years-old.

'Hello,' said Sarah with a smile. 'Are you lost?'

The young boy nodded, his eyes wide.

Sarah pulled a comical frowning face. 'Or are you a terrifying killer plant monster just taking the disguise of a lost little boy?'

'What?'

Jake rolled his eyes.

'I'm just looking for the toilet,' said the boy.

'You've come the wrong way,' said Sarah kindly. 'Head back towards the pool, and you'll see them out there, next door to the drinks kiosk.

With a brief nod, the boy turned and ran—just as a rousing cheer rang out.

'We should get back to the pool, too,' Sarah said. 'That's Liam's first race over.'

But Jake didn't move. He was scowling. 'What if that boy really *was* the Creeper, come to charge himself up—and he was surprised to see that we'd found his secret lair? We might have just let him slip through our fingers!'

Sarah sighed. 'Jake Latchford,' she said, pushing him towards the exit. 'You need to get more sleep!'

They returned to find the Larkspur Lions crowding round their four relay swimmers and hugging them tightly. The home side had clearly won the first race of the day.

'Hey, Liam!' called Jake to his friend, certain he was somewhere in the middle of the throng. 'You just missed it—Sarah and I found a secret room which might be—'

But Liam didn't respond. He was too busy giving and receiving high-fives from his team-mates to pay any attention.

Another announcement rang out over the crackly tannoy speaker: 'Would both teams now take their positions for the 400 metres freestyle.'

'You're up, Jenni!' Jake heard Liam say to a petite

Lions girl, now tucking her long hair beneath a golden swimming cap. 'Bring another win back for the team, eh?'

'You missed the race,' Liam said, finally turning to Jake.

'Not all of it,' protested Jake. 'I saw the bit when you dived in. That was brilliant!'

The man with the starting pistol and the still-damp suit stepped between them. 'I'm going to have to ask all non-swimmers to clear the end of the pool,' he said flatly, shooting a glance at Jake. 'Unless, of course, you're planning on knocking one of the coaches to the ground and accusing them of being The Riddler from Batman?'

'Ha!' chuckled Jake, reddening. 'No, of course I'm not. I'll just . . . I'll be . . .' He stood on tiptoe to look back at Liam over the man's shoulder. 'I'll give you a call tomorrow.'

Liam nodded, then grabbed a towel and sat with the rest of his team on their bench.

'I thought I had him, then,' Jake sighed as he rejoined Sarah at their spot and lay down again.

'Had who?' asked Sarah, almost to herself. 'The Creeper, or Liam as a friend again?'

31

It was another four days before Jake and Liam eventually met up.

Jake was out walking Max, and secretly checking every garden he passed for evidence of a petrifying plant person. The Creeper hadn't been officially spotted for several weeks now, and the longer it took for the monster to show himself, the more concerned Jake became.

And the worse his nightmares became.

He had just finished peering behind the hedge of the nearest front garden, when he spotted someone in a gold tracksuit and swimming cap walking down the centre of the street towards him.

Jake squinted. No . . . The person wasn't walking. They were swimming. With their arms, at least. They were doing front stroke with the top half of their body—including lifting their head to breathe at regular intervals—but marching along with a confident stride in the leg department.

'Liam?' said Jake. 'Is that you?'

Liam stopped a few metres from Jake and pulled off his swimming cap. If anything, his bleached hair reflected the sun even more than the gold rubber of his tight-fitting hat.

'Hiya,' said Liam. 'What's up?'

'Not much,' said Jake. 'You out for a swim, then?'

Liam looked around the sun-cracked tarmac of the

street. 'No,' he said, shaking his head. 'We're in the street, and there's no water here. That's one of the first things they teach you at swimming club—you need water to swim.'

'Oh, right,' said Jake with a chuckle. 'I thought it would have been something like, "You don't talk about swimming club!"'

'That would be ridiculous,' said Liam, frowning. 'We'd never get any new members if we were banned from talking about it.' His eyes lit up. 'Which reminds me . . .'

'No,' said Jake, raising a hand. 'I'm not joining the Larkspur Lions swimming club.'

'Why not?' demanded Liam. 'It's great fun, lots of exercise, and a good deal more exciting than spending your entire summer scouring people's gardens for a creature who may well be hundreds of miles away by now.'

'At least scouring gardens is better than pretending to swim up the middle of the road,' Jake protested. 'You look daft, man!'

'I've told you, I'm not swimming—or pretending to swim—I'm *exercising*.'

'For what?'

'The next lot of races!' replied Liam, flexing his arms. 'Toning up these bad boys could mean the difference between the incredible glory of the first place rosette,

33

and the bleak, depressing heartbreak of second place.'

'I hadn't thought of it like that,' said Jake.

'Not many people have,' said Liam. 'It was all my idea. The team was sceptical at first, but now they're all doing it. At least, that's what they've told me ...'

'And this is the same team you expect me to join?'

Liam smiled, pulling a bottle of bright blue liquid from the pocket of his shorts. 'Exactly! We've had another swimmer drop out with illness.' He spun the cap from the bottle and downed half the contents in one go.

'I'm not surprised, if you're all drinking stuff like that,' said Jake, looking disgusted.

Liam studied the front of the bottle. 'Nah, this stuff is really good for us athletes. Loads of essential vitamins, minerals, carbs ...'

'. . . and chock full of blue colouring, extra-sugary bubbles, and all the vital chemicals some bored scientist could cram into one small bottle,' finished Jake.

'That's the idea,' grinned Liam.

'If you don't mind, I'll stick to drinking basic water.'

Liam shuddered. 'Yuck! Rather you than me, mate!'

'So, who's dropped out now?'

'Arran Matthews—our top backstroker, no less. And I seem to recall from old PE lessons that the backstroke is a bit of a speciality of yours ...'

Jake's cheeks flushed in the heat. 'I'm not too bad at

it, yeah.'

'Then sign up!' Liam urged. 'You can't be having a good time just dragging Max around, looking for monsters. He certainly doesn't look as though he's having much fun.'

Jake looked down at his dog, who had taken the opportunity to lie down in the shade of a garden hedge for a quick nap.

'It's not proving to be the most exciting school holiday I've ever had,' Jake admitted.

'Then, you're in!' Liam cried as he flung his arms around his friend to hug him. 'The next practice—in water—is tonight, after the pool closes to the public at seven o'clock. I'll meet you there, and bring you a tracksuit. You just need trunks and a towel.'

Liam pulled his cap back on and turned to swim away.

Jake grabbed his arm to stop him.

'What?' asked Liam.

'Alright, I'll do it,' said Jake. 'I'll swim in your team. But, I have one condition . . .'

'What?!'

'Under absolutely no circumstances am I bleaching my hair!'

LARKSPUR LIDO
Summer Swimming Gala

LARKSPUR LIONS vs. MALTHAM MANTA RAYS

2 P.M. 3 AUGUST

RACES:

* 4 x 50m front crawl relay * 50m front crawl
* 50m breaststroke * 100m backstroke
* 100m butterfly * 200m individual medley

—

PLUS, ENTERTAINMENT ...

Tony Waggoner and his Musical Jam Jars

Mr Presto's Magic Show (featuring Clive the Spanish rabbit)

The Sharon Ramsbottom Dance Experience

—

Get your face painted!

Be a clown, a tiger, or a cheese board
(other designs available)

—

JUNIOR SWIMMERS!

Join the Splish Splashers Gang for fun in the kiddy pool!
Play amazing games such as water golf, funny
bubbles, and wet wipes—all in the company of Pirate
Captain Storm and his sidekick, Silly Sally.

GROWN-UPS—LEARN TO SWIM!

Come along and meet host of top TV game show *Can't
Swim, Won't Swim*, Larkspur's own Pepper Tempest. She
will help to banish your fear of water forever!

—

Vegan buffet provided by Mr Irving Campion of
Larkspur High School.

MENU:

* Pea and lettuce crepes
* Cucumber curry
* Oven-roasted tofu
* Wild mushroom surprise
* Hint of soup
* Celery

—

FOR MORE INFORMATION, CALL LARKSPUR LIDO
OR VISIT OUR STAND ON THE SECOND FLOOR OF
BUMBLEDALE'S SHOPPING CENTRE IN THE TOWN.

CHAPTER FIVE

CHANGING

Jake arrived at the lido a few minutes after seven o'clock, and was surprised to see the place open for business and the pool filled with excited kids and adults relaxing on loungers. He spotted Liam hanging around with his bleach-blonde buddies and made his way in their direction.

'Hey!' Liam cried as his friend approached. 'You made it! Jake, this is everyone . . . Everyone, this is Jake.'

'Has he come to attack another race starter?' asked one boy, a lad who looked far too big to be taking part in a children's swimming team. The shiny gold material of his tracksuit was barely able to stretch over his bulging muscles. And it was difficult to tell where the boy's neck ended and his face began.

Jake forced a smile at the comment. 'Just a case of mistaken identity,' he said. 'It won't happen again.'

Liam led him aside. 'Don't worry about Lurch,' he said quietly. 'He's fast in the water, but not the sharpest sandwich in the box when he's out on dry land.'

Jake blinked. 'Sharpest sandwich? I don't think that's . . .'

'So,' said Liam, interrupting. 'Got all your gear?'

Jake gestured to the rolled up towel beneath his arm. 'All present and correct.'

'Cool!' said Liam, grabbing a plastic carrier bag from the bench. 'This is the official Larkspur Lions golden tracksuit and swimming cap—all freshly washed and disinfected since Arran Matthews took to his sick-bed . . .'

Jake reached out for the bag, but Liam didn't hand it over.

'. . . and which will be awarded to the selected swimmer after this evening's try-outs.'

'Try-outs?' repeated Jake with a frown. 'I thought you said I could just come down and join?'

'If it was all down to me, mate, then yes—that's what would happen,' said Liam. 'But, we're on a winning streak at the moment. I can hardly bring in a new team member by saying "he's a cracking swimmer,

39

lads—honest!", can I?'

'Fair enough,' grumbled Jake. 'Although half of this lot look like they'll be flat on their backs by this time tomorrow.'

'How do you mean?'

'Look at them,' said Jake, gesturing to the team. 'At one end of the bench, you've got all your bleached bonces and tanned torsos. They *look* like they're ready to race. The Lions at the other end of the bench, however, look like they're ready to take part in a mass vomit, should anyone accidentally say the wrong word.'

Liam looked from one group to the other, and back again. 'Yeah, they do look pretty sickly,' he admitted. 'Maybe we'll be looking for more than one swimmer tonight, after all.'

'That's another thing,' said Jake. 'You told me the pool would be closed to the public.'

'It is,' said Liam.

Jake turned to look at the packed pool for a second. 'Er . . .'

'Oh.' His friend grinned. 'We don't train in that pool. That's just for visitors and races.'

'There's another pool?'

Liam nodded. 'On the other side of the seating. It's where we do all our training. If you get changed quickly enough, you could nip up and get a look at it.'

'Oh OK,' said Jake, sliding into one of the small changing cubicles at the side of the pool. He wished he'd brought a tracksuit of his own along, especially when he realized he'd managed to pick the smallest of his three pairs of swimming trunks out of the drawer. They felt—and looked—very tight indeed.

Emerging back out into the evening sunlight, he hoped no one was watching as he climbed the stairs at the sides of the raked seating. Perching on the top row, he peered down at a slightly smaller pool on the other side.

'Whoa! How old were you when your trunks last fitted properly?' demanded a voice.

Jake jumped. Sarah was standing right behind him.

'Don't!' he hissed. 'I picked up the wrong ones. Do they look really bad?'

'Not if you're trying to get a spot on the under-sevens team,' Sarah grinned.

Jake felt his cheeks flush red.

'Don't worry,' said Sarah, rooting through the rucksack at her feet. 'Here's one of Liam's spare pairs.'

Jake raised his eyebrows.

'Why are you carrying his swimming shorts around in your bag?'

'This is *his* bag,' said Sarah, giving it a shake. 'Liam says he doesn't trust the lockers here in case the other

41

teams bug them to try and find out the Lions' team tactics.'

'Aren't those tactics just "get in the water, swim faster than the other guy"?' asked Jake.

'You'd think so, wouldn't you?'

'Maybe not with your brother,' said Jake. 'Now, turn round so I can get changed under my towel, I'm not walking around the pool in these again!'

Sarah did as she was told, turning back when she heard: 'Ooh, that's better!'

'More your size?'

Jake nodded. He tied the cord around the waistband, then wriggled around in his seat. 'I just have to work some feeling back into my bum now. It's gone numb.' As he wriggled, he turned his attention back to the training pool. 'Is it me, or does the water down there look strange?'

'Strange?'

'Yeah . . . like, an unusual colour. A bit too *green* . . .'

Sarah's eyes widened. 'Don't start all that again,' she warned.

'I'm not, really!' said Jake, raising his hands in submission. 'It's just that, if you look at the public pool down there with people splashing about, having fun . . . Clear water, maybe with a hint of blue. Yes?'

'OK,' said Sarah, warily.

42

'Then look back at the training pool, and tell me the water down there doesn't look distinctly, well, green?'

'Hey, he's right,' said Liam as he reached the top of the seating area and joined them. 'The training pool does look pretty green from up here. I've never noticed that.'

Sarah compared the two separate swimming pools, as requested. 'Alright,' she said with a sigh. 'The water in the training pool does look a *little* more towards the vegetative end of the spectrum, but that could be down to all sorts of reasons.'

'Of course!' said Jake.

'And none of which have anything to do with me peeing in it!' announced Liam. 'No sir, not at all. Never done that. Apart from the one time, when I was desperate, of course. Oh, and when it started to rain and I couldn't get out of the water.'

'You couldn't get out of the water?' asked Jake.

'I told you,' said Liam. 'It was raining. I didn't want to get all wet, did I?'

'No,' said Jake. 'Of course not. Makes perfect sense.'

Sarah shook her head and looked away. 'If it's any comfort, Liam,' she said, 'I don't think the water looks green because you peed in it on two—'

'Six.'

'—six separate occasions.'

43

'Possibly seven. Ten at the most.'

Jake sighed. 'Was that just an empty pool before you started to pee in it? Have your teammates been training in a swimming pool filled entirely with your wee?'

'No!' scoffed Liam. 'Don't be daft! And before you ask, yes, someone from the water board comes out regularly to run tests in both these pools, and the little kids' paddling pool. Especially once people started falling ill.'

'And?'

'All perfectly safe to swim in,' Liam assured his friend.

Jake looked satisfied. 'I'm pretty sure the chlorine or whatever they use to keep the water clean will have dealt with something as strong as your wee by now.'

'Unless that's what's caused the discolouration,' said Sarah.

Jake and Liam looked to her expectantly.

'Well, if the cleaners put extra doses of hydrogen peroxide and chlorine in the pool, then one can easily cancel the other out. The result—murky green water, like that.'

Liam forced his gaping mouth to close. 'How on Earth do you know that?' he demanded.

Sarah waved her phone in their direction. 'Because

while you two were busy discussing the finer points of urine, I was looking up possible causes that could happen in the real world.'

'So, it definitely wasn't my wee?' said Liam.

'One hundred per cent certain,' his sister assured him.

'What if it's some kind of creepy weed monster?' asked a voice.

The trio froze.

Callum Ball—the closest thing they had to an arch enemy—was sitting behind them.

'How long have you been there?' asked Jake.

Callum shrugged. 'Long enough to hear that Liam likes relieving himself in the murky waters of the training pool,' he said. 'But then, who doesn't?'

'I don't think I will be,' muttered Jake.

'You have to get in the team first, Latchford!' said Callum, lifting up his T-shirt to reveal that he was also wearing swimming trunks.

Jake spun on Liam. 'You invited Callum to try out too?'

'It wasn't my fault,' Liam protested. 'CJ, the coach, said we each had to ask two people. But you were my first choice.'

'Thanks,' said Jake. 'That means a lot.'

'First or second choice, it doesn't matter,' said

45

Callum leaning back in his seat. 'It's all down to the results in this evening's races.'

'And you're still doing them?' Sarah asked.

'Of course!' said Callum. 'Why wouldn't I be?'

'Even if there's—what did you say—"some kind of creepy weed monster" in the pool?'

Callum laughed, but it looked strained. 'I'm just mucking about with you,' he exclaimed. 'Although . . .'

As Jake, Liam, and Sarah watched him, all the cockiness drained from Callum's expression and suddenly he looked scared, vulnerable.

'What is it?' asked Jake.

'I . . . I've been having these . . . these bad dreams,' Callum admitted, his eyes flickering as they probed some unseen memory.

Jake edged forward on his seat. 'What kind of bad dreams?'

Callum shrugged. 'I can't really remember them when I wake up,' he said, 'but I know they've scared me. And that they're all about some kind of bizarre plant monster.'

The trio exchanged glances, but said nothing.

'It's like I'm being chased by this thing—whatever it is—and it lashes out at me with long, I dunno . . . vines, I suppose. And then one of them catches me by the ankle, and it drags me to the ground. I think he's going to eat me ... and that's when I wake up.'

'What did it look like, this monster?' said Sarah.

'That's just it,' said Callum. 'Apart from the vines and the wooden teeth, the only other thing I can remember are these weird eyes. Weird, glowing green eyes.'

Then, as quickly as it went, Callum's tough attitude returned. It was like someone flipped his arrogant switch back to the 'on' position.

'So, let's just hope that's what's waiting for you at the bottom of that pool tonight, Jakey boy!' Jumping up, he paused only to slap Jake across the back of the head, then he headed for the stairs. 'Now, if you will excuse me, I'm off to do a hundred press-ups to get warmed up!'

Once he was out of earshot, Jake turned back to Liam and Sarah. 'That,' he said slowly, 'was bizarre.'

'You're telling me!' said Liam. 'Who does press-ups to get ready for a swimming race?'

'Not that,' sighed Jake. 'Callum has just described the exact same dream I've been having lately.'

'Weird,' said Liam. 'I bet no one ever has my frequent dream about going to Hong Kong to play ping pong against King Kong.'

'No, Liam. But Callum *was* captured by the Creeper when we went on the school camping trip,'

Jake reminded his friends.

'He was supposed to have amnesia and not remember any of that,' Sarah pointed out.

'Maybe he does remember it, deep down in his subconscious,' Jake suggested.

Before anyone could comment further, a whistle blew down near the training pool. They looked down to see that the coach was gathering both the current swimming team and the newcomers together there.

'That's us,' said Liam. He gave Jake a hearty pat on the back. 'This is your chance, mate. I know you can do it!'

Jake smiled, for real this time. 'Thanks.'

'No problem. Hey, and nice taste in swimming trunks too. I've got a pair exactly like those!'

CHAPTER SIX

GREEN

Jake joined the other potential team members and CJ, the Larkspur Lions' coach, at the shallow end of the training pool. In addition to him and Callum, there were two other swimmers vying to become a part of the local team—Ameena and Paul—both in the year above them at Larkspur High School.

Down at the edge of the pool, the colour of the water was even more pronounced than it had been from above. Maybe the rays of the early evening sun were adding a golden tint to the surface, but Jake was certain there was a deep yellow sheen glistening on top of the water. He tried not to think about how many times Liam had peed in there.

'OK,' said CJ, 'Gather round.'

The swimmers did as they were instructed and spent the next ten minutes listening to a brief history of the Larkspur Lions, and what the team expected of new members.

'This race will be two lengths of the pool,' the coach informed them. 'Front crawl only. Remember, this is slightly smaller than the public pool over there where we hold our races, so the turns could come up a lot sooner than you think. You'll need to be ready for that for when we're competing away from home too. So, let's see what you can do in the water.'

The four swimmers took a moment to stretch their muscles, then they each found a place at the edge of the pool. Jake was in lane two, with Callum to his left and the two others taking up lanes three and four.

A hush fell over the practice area, and the sound of young families enjoying their time in and around the main pool seemed to fade away into the distance. Trying to calm his nerves, Jake took a few deep breaths and tried to clear his mind of the events of the past week or two. Despite his bad dreams and the occasional case of mistaken identity, there had been no real sightings of the Creeper since the summer holidays had started.

Maybe Woody had gone into hiding or, better still, moved on to another town. No, he wouldn't wish that on anyone else, even if it did rid Larkspur of the problem. With any luck, the Creeper had lost his powers and he was permanently human again. Or perhaps Woody had pushed one of his transformations too far and was now stuck in plant form. How long could he live for, then? There was an oak tree outside his school that had been there for hundreds of years.

Jake shivered at the thought. He didn't like the idea of the Creeper being practically immortal.

CJ stepped into view at the side of the pool, the starting pistol clutched in his hand. 'On your marks . . .' he called out.

Jake blinked hard; something was making his eyes sting and he wished that he had remembered to bring his swimming goggles with him. Callum, Paul, and Ameena were wearing theirs. He briefly considered calling up to Liam—still sitting in the raised seating area with Sarah—to ask if he could borrow a pair. But everyone else seemed ready to get going and he didn't want to cause any delays. Doing so wouldn't earn him any brownie points from the coach, and it had taken long enough for the teasing about his recent attack on the race starter to die down. He'd never get on the team if he got a reputation for being a troublemaker.

'Get set . . .'

This was it. Jake's chance to forget about monsters

and fill his summer with sunshine and swimming instead. Despite his earlier reservations, he suddenly felt determined to win a place on the Larkspur Lions team.

BANG!

All four swimmers hit the water at the same time. Jake's strongest swimming stroke was the backstroke, but he understood why the coach would want to test the entrants equally and so they were all restricted to the front crawl. Surfacing from the initial dive, he took in a deep lungful of air then plunged his face back into the water and swam as hard and as fast as he could.

It was a few seconds later when he realized that his eyes weren't stinging any longer—they were burning. Whatever was discolouring the water was doing the same thing to his eyes, only turning them red instead of a disturbing shade of lime green. He'd have to be careful not to swallow any of the stuff. Who knew what it would do to your insides?

He risked glances left and right to see if the other three swimmers were affected as well, but they were all wearing goggles. And they were starting to pull ahead . . .

Trying to ignore the pain in his eyes, Jake dug deep into his reserves of energy and picked up some speed. While he wanted to qualify for the team, it was just as important to him—if not more—that he beat Callum.

It wasn't so much that Callum was a bully—he wasn't quite big enough, or dumb enough for that. He was just, well . . . annoying! Wherever he went these days, Callum always seemed to be waiting to make his life a—

THUMP!

Jake hit his head against the end wall of the swimming pool. Hard. He'd had his eyes screwed shut to try and ease the sensation of fire burning the inside of his eyeballs. CJ had warned them to watch out for the turn, too.

Jake planted his feet against the offending wall and pushed off for the final length, hoping that no one else had seen what had happened.

He looked up to see Callum smirking at him before his head plunged back under the water.

Yep. He'd seen.

Callum pulled away, almost certain to win the race now. Jake gritted his teeth and forced himself to make up the distance between them. He knew he was likely to suffer for the extra effort the following day, but aching muscles would be nothing compared to Callum's derisive comments. Plus, his head already hurt from colliding with the concrete side of the pool. What were a few more aches and pains in the pursuit

53

of swimming glory?

The two other swimmers were still lagging behind Jake, and he was slowly gaining on Callum. Was it possible to catch up with his rival now? Or, at the very least, would the team coach be impressed with his recovery and comeback, following his collision?

Suddenly, something under the water grabbed hold of his leg.

It was long, thin, and snakelike, and it was wrapping itself around Jake's ankle, making it difficult for him to kick his legs.

Jake spun in the water, to try to catch a glimpse of what had hold of his leg but, thanks to his sore eyes, all he could make out was a long tendril fixed around his ankle and twisting its way further up his body.

A tendril? Was the Creeper in the water with them? Had Callum been right about weeds lurking at the bottom of the pool?

He tried to shout out a warning to his fellow swimmers, receiving a mouthful of water for his efforts as he twisted round, trying to grab the tendril before it could climb further up his body.

Suddenly, he felt the thin vine slip between his fingers, and he pulled as hard as he could. The tendril came away, and Jake thrust his fist into the air, ready to toss what remained of the terrible green vegetation on to the tiled waterside—when he recognized it as the cord from a pair of swimming trunks.

Gah!

Looking up, he saw that his rival had already completed the race and was waiting at the end of the pool with a cheesy grin plastered over his face. Gritting his teeth, Jake pressed on, heading for the finish—the end of the cord still clinging to his ankle.

Paul and Ameena reached the finish line just seconds after Jake, but he wasn't too concerned about them. All he could think about was that he'd come in

55

second. To Callum.

And there stood Callum, at the edge of the pool, holding out a hand to help Jake out of the water. Jake was about to slap the offered hand away when he saw the coach watching them carefully. He would not only want the strongest swimmers to join the Larkspur Lions, but also those who appeared to be gracious team players.

Swallowing his anger, Jake accepted Callum's hand and allowed himself to be helped out of the pool. He stepped up to the race winner, blinking hard as his eyes continued to sting.

'Congratulations,' he said through gritted teeth. 'And thanks.'

Callum flashed his most annoying, self-satisfied grin. 'Anytime! Shame about your little, er, accidents out there . . .'

'Yeah,' said Jake. Reaching down, he unwrapped the length of cord from his leg and tossed it aside.

'Hey, that's mine!' said Lurch, retrieving the wet string. 'I wondered where I'd lost it.'

'OK, then . . .' said CJ, scanning through the notes he'd made on his clipboard.

The boys turned to face him.

Jake's muscles began to ache as he walked home. But it wasn't a good ache, like he might feel if he'd spent an afternoon playing football, or been out cycling with Liam and Sarah. This was a dull throb which seemed to envelop his whole body, like he was coming down with the flu. And he felt queasy.

He hoped he hadn't caught a bug from swimming in the green-tinted water. Paul and Ameena had complained of not feeling very well as they left the lido earlier. Jake didn't fancy spending the rest of the summer being ill and stuck in bed, like those kids who'd already had to drop out of the swimming team.

Not that it really mattered. CJ had only made him one of the reserves. Jake wouldn't be swimming alongside Liam, even after all that effort. He'd spend each gala sitting on a bench, in his golden tracksuit, next to the pasty kids with asthma, all of them just waiting for one of the main team to pull a muscle and give them a chance at competing.

He turned to cross a patch of open ground; a shortcut that would cut a good ten minutes from his walk home. Suddenly, his T-shirt caught on one of the twisted branches of the tree and he was jerked backwards. Brilliant! That was all he needed—a hole in his top that he'd have to explain to his mum when he got home.

Jake dropped his bag to the sun-cracked soil and twisted round, trying to see where he'd caught himself. If he could get free without causing too much damage ...

'I hear you've been ssseeing me in your dreamsss, boy!' hissed a voice in his ear.

Jake froze. This wasn't just any tree that had snagged his T-shirt. It was the Creeper! He swallowed hard.

'What do you want?' he demanded.

The voice cackled—that chilling noise that sounded like a rusty saw cutting through rotten wood.

'You know jussst what I want, child!' the creature breathed. 'I want plantsss to take over the Earth, to rule in place of humansss ...'

Jake tugged at the collar of his T-shirt, no longer caring if he tore the material or not. But the Creeper's grip held him tight, its long twig-fingers extending to caress the skin of his neck as he struggled.

'But, I'm just a kid,' Jake croaked. 'I can't give you that power.'

'And I'm not asssking you for it,' rasped the Creeper. 'You're jussst the ssstart. You will be the firssst of many pathetic humansss who will be made in my image.'

'No chance!' spat Jake, reaching up to grab the branch at his throat. He wrapped his fist around the gnarled wood and pulled down as hard as he could, snapping the stick in two.

The Creeper screamed in pain—a noise far worse than his laughter—and Jake was free. Snatching up his bag, he ran across the deserted space, stumbling over broken bricks and crumbling clumps of concrete.

He didn't stop running until he had reached the corner of his street. Only then did Jake dare pause to catch his breath and check behind him to see if he was being pursued.

Thankfully, he was alone. The pain he had inflicted on the Creeper must have been enough to cause him to abandon the chase.

And now Jake's muscles really were aching!

'The reserve team?' said Jake's dad that evening as he smeared a dollop of thick, green, home-made vegetable spread over a piece of crusty bread. 'That's not bad.'

Jake sat at the kitchen table, staring into the distance.

But he couldn't shake the sound of the Creeper's

scream from his mind. While he was glad he'd managed to cause the creature some pain, he knew the piercing shriek was likely to fuel his nightmares for many nights to come.

'Jake!' said his dad, a little louder this time. 'I said being a reserve isn't bad.'

'Of course it's bad!' countered Jake, allowing himself to be pulled back to reality. 'It means that Callum got on to the first team. I'll have to go along to all the swimming contests and cheer him on.'

His dad shrugged. 'So don't do it, then.'

'I can't pull out now,' said Jake. 'Everyone will think I'm sulking because I didn't make the first team.'

'Isn't that what's happening?' said Dad with a wink.

'No,' said Jake. 'I'm not sulking. I'm . . .'

'Jealous?'

'Jealous of Callum Ball?' scoffed Jake. 'Of course not!'

Dad said nothing and took a big bite of his pungent snack.

'Well, alright, maybe I'm a *little* bit jealous,' Jake continued. 'I thought joining the swimming team would be a good way to hang out with Liam again. But now, everywhere we go, that cheat is always going to be there.'

'You don't know for certain that he cheated,' Dad

pointed out. 'It may not have been *his* trunks cord that got caught around your leg.'

'Do you have to eat that stuff?' Jake asked. 'It reeks!'

'Delicious, though!' his dad replied, offering Jake a hearty thumbs up. 'And, I get all of my five a day in only twelve servings! You should try some.'

Jake shuddered. 'I think I'd rather share Max's food, thanks.'

The back door opened and Jake's mum came in, carrying an empty kettle. 'Nope,' she said. 'None of the neighbours have got any running water, either.'

Jake hurried over to catch the door before it could swing shut. He stood on the doorstep, breathing in the fresh night air, hoping the breeze would ease his still painful eyes, but also warily watching the branches of the neighbours' trees as they wafted in the evening breeze.

Mum crossed to the sink to try the taps one more time. Nothing came out. 'The water board have probably cut it off at the mains to work on the problem we've been having.'

'What problem?' Jake asked.

'Oh, the water's been playing up since this morning,' his mum said. 'It smells horrible, and comes out a murky green colour. Some people have been boiling it to use, but I wasn't sure, so I've not touched the stuff.'

61

'Tell me about it,' said Dad. 'I'd kill for a cup of tea!'

'I was about to make you one,' said Mum. 'Well, I was about to make one for Jake to say well done for getting on the swimming team...'

'Reserve swimming team,' Jake pointed out.

'You should still be proud of an achievement like that. And your dad would have got a cup of tea out of it, so he'd have no reason to complain, either.'

'What about juice?' said Dad. 'That's not green as well, is it?'

'No, it's not!' said Mum, hurrying to the fridge. 'Three glasses of congratulatory orange juice coming up!'

As Jake watched his mum pour out the drinks, he rested his head back against the doorframe and thought about the swimmers who had been forced out of the swimming team after they had fallen ill. Were they victims of whatever was contaminating the water supply? How was the Creeper causing it? And would he be struck down by it, too?

The answer would have to wait until the water was turned back on and, even then, he didn't fancy using himself as a guinea pig in any kind of experiment to find out.

CHAPTER SEVEN

PRACTICE

The first scheduled swimming practice had been arranged for two days later. Jake spent the intervening time reading, playing *Brick-Quest* on his computer, or taking Max on long, rambling walks around the town. Anything to keep his mind occupied and to stop him dwelling on the fact that no one else seemed to believe the Creeper was back and plotting something big.

He'd gone next door to tell his friends about his latest encounter with the monster but, no matter how much they nodded and sympathised, Jake could tell they didn't believe him.

After a while, Jake began to doubt his own memory. He'd been thinking about the Creeper on the walk back home from the lido. Was it possible he'd just got tangled up in the branches of a tree and imagined the rest? He had no proof that the encounter had ever happened, apart from a small tear in one of his favourite T-shirts.

Eventually, he decided to keep the story to himself. He didn't want his mates to think he was going bonkers any more than they already suspected.

On the morning of training, he stopped at the shop on the corner of Duncan Street to buy a few bottles of water, tucking two into his kit bag, but holding the third up to the cloudless sky as he stepped back out into the sun.

After so many days of green tinged liquid spraying out of the taps at home it seemed strange to see clear water again, and he had almost finished the bottle as he arrived at the lido.

Jake was a little nervous, hoping that word of his trial wouldn't have spread among the rest of the team. He didn't want to spend the summer being the butt of everyone's jokes just because he'd fallen for one of Callum's stupid pranks.

But no one seemed to pay him any attention when he arrived at the changing rooms. The team had competed against the Sherrinford Sharks the night before, and several team members were parading around the room with the medals and trophies they had won.

Jake noticed that the winners all seemed to be those with bleached blonde hair, some of whom now also seemed to have a faint green tint to their skin. The result of spending too much time in the badly-filtered training pool, no doubt.

'Hey!' said Liam, sliding on to the bench beside Jake. 'I was hoping you'd be there last night, to watch us swim to glory!' He waved a glistening golden medal in front of his friend's face to illustrate his point.

Jake grinned. 'Sorry,' he said, 'Dad had to go out, so there was no one to give me a lift. And, mate or no mate, I'm not sitting on the bus to Sherrinford for over an hour each way just to watch your blond bonce bob up and down in the water.'

'You should see their pool,' said Liam. 'Talk about fancy! Heated water, racing lanes marked out . . .'

'. . . no underwater tentacles to grab your legs as you swim,' added a second voice.

The boys turned to discover Callum sitting on the other side of Jake.

'Yep,' said Jake, forcing a smile now that his natural good mood had faded. 'You got me the other day. Nice work!'

'Just a bit of teammate banter,' said Callum.

'Except that, because of it, I didn't get on the team,'

65

Jake pointed out. 'I'm in the reserves.'

'Count yourself lucky,' said Liam. 'The reserve team gets to practise in the main pool with the public around them. Us lot will be stuck swimming up and down the green lagoon!'

'Yeah,' said Jake, thinking of how many times he'd have to dodge around younger kids screaming and belting each other with inflatable toys all morning. 'I'm really lucky.'

'But first,' said Liam, 'we've got CJ's pre-swim warm up to get through ...'

Jake frowned. 'Pre-swim warm up?'

By the time he was approaching the end of his fourth lap running around Larkspur Lido, Jake was certain that everyone could see his heart pounding in and out beneath his T-shirt. This was a nightmare! Their coach's idea of a 'bit of light exercise to get the body working' wouldn't have been out of place at an army Special Forces assault course!

They'd started with a series of simple stretches, which Jake had actually enjoyed. And he hadn't really been fazed by the sets of lunges and squats that followed. The sit-ups had proved to be more difficult—especially as everyone else had several weeks' head start on him in terms of practice. But by the time the press-ups came around, his muscles were screaming for mercy.

'This . . . is . . . torture!' he wheezed to Liam as they rounded the ticket-office end of the lido for the fifth time. 'Even Mr Davison's PE lessons at school aren't this bad!'

Liam chuckled. 'Yeah, CJ's a bit of a tough boss,' he said.

'What's happened to you?' Jake demanded of his friend. 'You used to *hate* any kind of exercise or activity apart from lunchtime football!'

'I've seen the light, Jakey-boy!' smirked Liam. 'All this running and swimming and stuff is a killer—but just imagine how fit I'll be when I take on those year nines again in September. At this rate, I could even make the school team! Plus, it's doing us good.'

'I hope so,' said Jake, 'because I don't think I'm going to be able to move for the next few days.'

'When we first started, CJ used to get everyone at the lido involved in his warm-ups,' said Liam. 'The public as well as the team! We got so many complaints, you'd think he was some sort of maniac.'

Jake stopped running and grabbed his friend's arm. 'What did you just say?'

67

Liam shrugged. 'What? That CJ tried to get everyone in town fit, along with the swimmers?'

'No, the bit about him being a maniac,' said Jake, squinting to the other end of the pool where the coach was shouting at each runner who passed, urging them to do better. 'You don't think he could be . . .'

'No, I don't!' said Liam flatly. Then he set off running again.

Jake sprinted to catch up. 'But, you've got to admit it's quite a coincidence that CJ is in charge of the bright green training pool . . .'

Liam sighed. 'I'd hoped getting you involved in the Larkspur Lions would give you something else to think about other than these insane conspiracy theories about the Creeper. But, it obviously hasn't.'

'No, it has,' countered Jake. 'It's just that . . . I know you don't believe me, but I really did see him the other night. He grabbed me as I was walking home. And then he chased after me. At least, I think he did . . .'

'You need to forget all that stuff and enjoy yourself,' said Liam with a look of concern. 'Come on . . .' Without waiting, Liam picked up speed to catch up with one of the other bleached-haired team members, Ben. He dropped into pace behind the boy and began to put him off his stride by playfully jabbing a finger in each of his sides in turn.

'Hey!' laughed Ben, trying to twist out of Liam's reach while continuing to run. 'Get off me, you idiot!'

Liam laughed, clearly having fun. He glanced back at Jake, then gestured to Barry—another runner—encouraging his friend to copy his actions.

But Jake wasn't in the mood for tickling games, especially as he was still very much the new boy on the team. Plus, he didn't want to get into CJ's bad books, just in case he was given extra laps to run.

Or even worse ...

Jake spent the rest of the morning swimming up and down in the main pool. He repeatedly glanced up at the clocks CJ had set up at either end of the water, timing himself and trying to complete each length just a few seconds faster than his previous attempt.

As he had predicted, trying to practise in a pool that was also open to members of the public was proving to be a challenge, at the very least. More than once, he'd collided with children clinging on to all manner of blow-up toys: whales, boats, and, for some strange reason, an inflatable vacuum cleaner.

Most of these kids just ignored him and continued

to play, unaware that they were blocking his path or slapping him in the face with the whale's tail. But one or two of the younger swimmers had taken it upon themselves to deliberately get in his way, or splash him as he passed.

The worst culprit was Noah, the boy with ginger hair who had been looking for the toilets a few days earlier. He seemed to have taken something of a dislike to Jake. This was to the point where he'd given up simple splashing and had fetched a rifle-sized Super Soaker water pistol from his mum's bag, and was using Jake for what could only be described as target practice.

The only other reserve training today—a girl whose name Jake didn't know—seemed to be avoiding unwanted attention by swimming close to the other edge of the pool. Jake had made an effort to join her in relative safety, but Noah had just jumped on the back of an inflatable sea-horse and paddled after him, filling the tanks of his Super Soaker as he swam.

So Jake was relieved when CJ appeared at the poolside, blowing his whistle to call him and his fellow reserve swimmer out of the water and around the seating to the shimmering, emerald training pool. Noah gave him one final blast to the back of his head to say goodbye.

If anything, the water looked an even more

alarming shade of green today—although that could be because the rest of the Larkspur Lions team were all lined up along the edges, each wearing a skin-tight lycra jumpsuit in a violent fluorescent lime colour.

'What's all this?' Jake whispered to Liam as he collected his own jumpsuit from CJ, and joined his friend in the line-up.

Liam struck a pose and beamed. 'Only a way to make me look utterly awesome!'

Jake stepped back to take in a full view of his friend in skin-tight lime green. 'You think so, do you?'

Liam nodded. 'Too right! It's like . . . You know that bloke who used to be a wrestler, but he's in the movies now?'

'The Rock?'

'That's him!' said Liam. 'I could be his sidekick!'

'What? The Pebble?'

'You can't mock it,' sneered Liam.

'I think I just did,' said Jake with a smile.

'Well, let's see how you look when you've got yours on . . .'

Jake turned the sleek material over in his hands. 'That's if I can get into the thing.'

'It is tricky,' admitted Liam. 'I got my foot caught in it as I was getting changed and it pinged back. I almost kicked myself in the face.'

'Right, that's enough chatter!' said CJ. 'Settle down . . .' He waited until the entire team was giving him their undivided attention, then began.

'You may be wondering why you're all dressed like this,' he said.

Jake briefly wondered if he should make a funny comment to get everyone laughing. Maybe the rest of the team would accept him more if he could make them giggle. It always worked for Liam, but he didn't want to end up doing extra laps of the lido for speaking out of turn. Instead he bit his lip and listened hard.

'These are known as "swim thins",' continued CJ, 'Or at least that's what I call them. They remove any friction from your swimming costume or even your own skin that could hold you back in the water.'

One or two of the more experienced swimmers ran their hands down the sleek material, nodding and smiling.

'In tests,' CJ went on, 'such suits have been known to increase swim times by up to four tenths of a second, and you know what a difference that can make . . .'

Again, Jake had to swallow the jokey comment he was eager to make to Liam. If the pair had been back in school, they'd be giggling like a pair of four-year-old girls by now.

'And best of all,' said CJ, adjusting the shoulders of his own swim thin, 'they are—at this moment—*not* banned by the rules of the sport at this level of competition!'

Jake couldn't help himself any longer. 'Yeah,' he said. 'That's only because the underwater fashion police haven't paid Larkspur a visit yet!'

No one laughed. No one at all. Not even Liam.

Jake felt his cheeks redden and burn.

'Do you have a comment you'd like to share with us about the swim thin I have personally bought for you out of my own pocket, Mr Latchford?' CJ grunted.

'No, sir,' said Jake, staring down at his toes, the skin still wrinkled from his morning in the pool.

'Good, then perhaps you'd like to go and change into yours and see if you can swim an entire race without believing that some underwater menace is trying to drag you below the surface.'

This time, the team did laugh. They laughed at Jake as he stomped away, not daring to look back at Liam in case he saw his best friend joining in with the hilarity.

The only good thing about the situation was he could now change into the lycra suit in private. Knowing his luck, he'd probably get tangled up in the material and catapult himself out of the window.

He slammed open the door to the changing room, which was empty aside from Callum who was already wearing his swim thin.

Oh great! thought Jake. *He's all I need right now!*

But Callum wasn't paying him any attention. Instead, he was staring into the mirror over the sink, examining his own tongue. And it was easy to see why—it was bright green.

'What happened to you?' Jake demanded.

'Nothing!' said Callum, pulling his tongue back in as quickly as he could.

'What?' said Jake. 'Aside from your bright green

tongue?'

'Oh, *that*?' said Callum, forcing a grin. 'That's just because I brought a bottle of limeade with me to drink today. Got to keep hydrated, Jakey-boy!'

Jake caught sight of the half-empty bottle of water in Callum's locker just as he slammed the small metal door and hurried for the exit.

That certainly wasn't limeade. In fact, he couldn't remember seeing the stuff on sale in any of the local shops for years now. Everyone bought cola or plain old water.

The thought made room for a nagging suspicion to slither inside Jake's mind and take hold . . .

Could Callum be the Creeper?

CHAPTER EIGHT

MOSS

'Get off me!'

Jake sat bolt upright in his bed, his sweat-soaked T-shirt clinging to his body. He sighed.

He'd had another nightmare about the Creeper.

Pulling off his damp top, he wondered whether Callum was also having bad dreams. And, if he was, why weren't Liam and Sarah complaining about a lack of sleep too? They'd witnessed the Creeper's terrifying tricks as well, but they didn't seem to be tormented by the rooted rotter, like he was.

However it was they were managing to keep calm, he wished they could teach him. They appeared to be determined to relax and enjoy the summer holidays, while Jake spent every waking moment—and many sleeping ones, too—worrying about where and when the Creeper would strike next.

The duvet at the foot of his bed started to wriggle around, and something licked one of Jake's feet. He felt confident enough that his adversary wasn't in bed with him to pull back the covers. The offender was, of course, Max.

'I knew you wouldn't be too far away,' chuckled Jake. He gave the dog a pat on the head before lying back down. But Max had other plans. He leapt over Jake's legs, trotted across the room, and rested a paw up against the door.

'You want to go out now?' groaned Jake, checking the time on his phone.

2.12 a.m.

Max gave a quiet *snuff* and padded back to the bed to lick his hand.

'Alright,' said Jake, wiping the slobber off on his pyjamas. He grabbed a dry T-shirt and pulled it on as he opened the bedroom door.

The pair made their way downstairs and into the darkened kitchen, where a sudden flash of green light made Jake stop suddenly. The eerie light lit up the entire wall for a second, then disappeared.

Then it was back. And gone again. Back. And gone again.

Could it be that the Creeper was somehow—

No, it was the clock on the microwave, flashing 12:00 on its black face. Jake allowed himself to breathe again as he remembered the short power cut they'd had earlier that evening. The clock just needed resetting.

Telling himself off for being so jittery, Jake unlocked the back door and pulled it open so that Max could nip out and take care of his business—only to find the Creeper stood waiting on their doorstep!

This time, there was no mistaking the piercing green of the monster's eyes, or the twisted, wooden arm that shot out towards Jake's throat.

'Get off me!' Jake cried, slamming the door closed and trapping the leafy limb. Outside, the Creeper screamed in pain; this was the same arm Jake had snapped the fingers off during their last encounter.

By his legs, Max started growling, his hackles raised as Jake fought to close the door. Jake looked along the kitchen counters for a weapon—but they were empty, all the knives were safely slotted into the wooden block near the far door. If he let go of this door to get one, the Creeper would be inside and on him before he was halfway across the room.

In fact, the only thing within reach was the remaining half of the French loaf his dad used to eat his homemade vegetable spread with. Grabbing the bread,

Jake began to batter it against the squirming arm of the beast that was desperate to get at him. The Creeper snarled and hissed as he pushed hard against the door.

Then the French loaf snapped in two, one half falling to the floor, the other still clutched in Jake's hand. He sighed. That hadn't worked at all.

He considered just pulling the door open and setting Max on the monster. Unlike Jake's previous encounters, Max hadn't run away at first sight of the Creeper. But what if the angry assailant actually hurt his dog? Jake didn't think he could live with that.

So, steeling himself, Jake wrapped his hands around the wrist of the Creeper's wooden limb. The feel of it turned his stomach; he could actually feel miniature rivers of liquid—presumably the sap the monster had running through his veins instead of blood—flowing beneath the rough bark of the beast's skin.

Breaking the creature's fingers had been enough to force him to abandon the last attack. There was no reason the same tactic wouldn't work again.

Anchoring his feet against the bottom of the door, Jake pulled back on the wooden limb as hard as he could.

There was a sickening CRACK, and the Creeper's arm ripped clean off, clattering to the floor beside Jake. The obstruction cleared, the door slammed shut, muting the monster's scream of pain.

Jake stared down at the broken appendage, half expecting it to display a life of its own and leap up at his throat. But it didn't. The wooden arm just lay there, unmoving and silent.

Just as silent as the garden now was, on the other side of the door.

Was that it? Had the Creeper run off, leaving his severed arm behind?

There was only one way to find out.

Cautiously Jake pushed down on the handle, and pulled the door open just far enough to peer through. The back garden appeared to be empty but, of course, the Creeper could be hiding in the shadows somewhere.

Taking a deep breath, Jake pulled the door open wide, striking a martial arts pose he'd learned from his *Brick-Quest* 'Ninja' add-on pack. He hoped the stance would be enough to stop the Creeper from attacking. But in the end, it didn't matter. The garden was silent. The Creeper had gone. The only evidence that it had ever been there was the lone gnarly limb, lying at his feet.

Gingerly, Jake picked up the severed arm and hurled it towards the bushes at the far end of the garden. Then he was nearly knocked to the ground as the furry blur of Max raced out after it.

'No, Max! Don't . . .'

But it was too late. Max already had the Creeper's arm in his mouth and was trotting back across the lawn towards the house, his tail wagging happily.

Leaping up the steps and into the kitchen, Max dropped the arm in front of Jake and sat down obediently, waiting for his human friend to throw the stick again.

Jake wiped a hand over his face. This really was going to be a long night . . .

'They're limiting everyone to two bottles each,' said Jake, dumping the bottled water into their supermarket trolley, alongside the rest of the shopping.

'Two each?' said his mum as she moved the bottles to the end of the trolley and tried to plump up the loaf of bread Jake had just squashed with them. 'That won't be enough. Although I did expect there would be a rush on the stuff at the moment.'

'There's a guy from the water board in the bottled drinks aisle,' Jake explained. 'He says our tap water is completely safe, even though it's discoloured.'

'But it stays green, even when you boil it,' Mum pointed out. 'It can't be good for you.'

Jake shrugged. 'That's why I think I should switch exclusively to cola until all this business ends. Leave the water for you and Dad . . .'

'Nice try, buster,' said Mum. 'But I don't fancy having you acting hyper twenty-four hours a day because you're full of fizzy pop, thank you very much!'

'What about ice?' asked Jake, suddenly.

'What about it?'

'Well, that's just frozen water, isn't it? If we bought a load of ice, we could let it melt and have more fresh water.'

Mum ruffled her hand through her son's mop of dark hair. 'Just when I think you're nothing but a buzzed up cola fiend! That's a great idea. Go and get some bags, but try to be subtle about it. We don't want to give away your brainwave.'

Jake nodded and set off for the tall freezers lined up against the far wall of the shop, collecting a basket en route. He worked his way past the stacks of ice cream and desserts to where the ice was, and found Liam standing in front of one of the freezers dressed in only his swim thin. The cabinet door was wide open.

'H-h-h-hello, m-m-mate!' Liam grinned.

Jake stared, speechless for a second. 'What in the name of all things *Brick-Quest* are you doing?'

'CJ s-said we had to get used to extremes in t-t-temperature, in case the w-weather turns bad on one of the race d-days,' Liam explained, closing the freezer door and jumping around to warm himself up.

'But, still . . .'

'I tried getting in the big chest freezer at home, but my mum said I wasn't allowed to bin the fish fingers in order to make enough room.'

'There's a few packs of burgers I won't ever be eating in there, as well,' said Sarah as she approached them. 'Not since you sat on them, anyway.'

Jake gestured to Liam. 'You knew he was doing this?'

Sarah shrugged. 'At this point I'm just hoping that him being my brother is some sort of big practical joke.'

Liam and Sarah helped Jake carry half a dozen bags of ice back to his mum's trolley and, once they had paid and loaded the car, he grabbed his swimming kit from the boot and the trio set off walking down to the lido for that day's training.

'So,' said Jake after a short while. 'I've got a theory about the Creeper . . .'

'Here we go again,' said Liam, sharing a weary

glance with his sister.

'Don't be like that!' said Jake. 'I'm the one in danger here!'

Sarah scowled. 'Danger? How?'

Jake took a deep breath. 'Would you believe me if I told you the Creeper tried to get in my house to attack me last night?'

Liam and Sarah glanced at each other, but said nothing.

'It's true!' Jake urged. 'I had to rip his arm off to scare him away.'

'And where's this arm now?' asked Sarah.

Jake sighed. 'Max wanted to play fetch with it so, in the end, I threw it over the fence into next door's garden. It's the only way I could get the dog to come inside.'

'You threw it into our garden?' exclaimed Liam, his eyes wide.

'Of course not!' said Jake. 'The one on the other side. Where Mrs Webb lives.'

'So, it should still be there,' said Sarah.

'No,' said Jake. 'I looked first thing this morning, and it had gone.'

Sarah thought for a second. 'Seems a bit convenient.'

'The Creeper probably wanted to stitch it back on,'

said Liam with a grin. 'You know—tree surgery!'

'Oh, ha ha,' said Jake. 'I knew you two wouldn't believe me.'

'That could be because you're seeing the Creeper everywhere,' explained Sarah. 'I know he can shapeshift into human form, but it's getting daft! First he's the guy starting the race at the Lido, then he's some kid trying to find the toilets. You'll be claiming it's me next!'

Jake shook his head. 'I'd never think it was you. Not now I'm certain that it's Callum.'

Liam stopped walking. 'Callum? Ball? From school?'

Jake nodded. 'And the swimming team,' he reminded them. 'Think about it—it's the perfect disguise. He gets to hang around the lido, with all that lovely algae to feed on, and there are plenty of ready victims around for whatever his latest evil scheme will be!'

Liam switched his kitbag to his other shoulder and continued walking. 'You've completely lost it. You know that, don't you?'

Jake glared at him. 'Says Freezer Boy . . .'

'You've got to admit it sounds a *bit* far-fetched,' said Sarah. 'He only joined the swimming team on the same day as you.'

'Yes,' Jake agreed, 'but he's been hanging around the lido for most of the summer. We're lucky he hasn't attacked anyone yet—us three especially.'

'Half of Larkspur has spent their summer at the lido!' said Sarah. 'Not only could the Creeper be any one of them, but he's hardly likely to attack us in public, is he?'

'Hey, you're not accusing Doris behind the counter in the cafe of being a crazed plant beast, are you?' asked Liam in mock horror. 'Actually, forget I said that. She doesn't need you marching in there, accusing her of growing military-grade tomatoes!'

'I don't need to accuse Doris of anything,' said Jake. 'I *know* the Creeper is Callum. Well, I'm fairly certain, anyway. Yesterday, he had a green tongue!'

'And I'm wearing green pants under this thing!' scoffed Liam. 'It doesn't mean my bum is plotting evil schemes! And I haven't noticed Callum doing so, either!'

'Alright, let's calm down for a minute,' said Sarah as the trio approached the lido. 'Jake is allowed to have his theories, and he's just trying to protect innocent people from being hurt. How about if the three of us agree to keep a close eye on Callum at today's swimming practice?'

'That's what I was planning to do, anyway,' said

Jake. 'You both promise you'll help?'

'Of course,' said Sarah, smiling. 'We'll watch Callum with you, won't we, Liam?'

Liam sighed. 'Actually, I haven't been one hundred per cent truthful with you ...'

'About what?' demanded Jake. 'You mean you *have* seen Callum acting suspiciously?'

'No,' replied Liam. 'It's about my green underpants. I'm actually not wearing any at all.'

The morning's swimming practice passed like any other. Liam and the rest of the main team raced up and down in the off-colour training pool, while Jake fought off the attention of the ginger-haired boy, who had turned up for target practice with an even bigger Super Soaker.

It was bad enough that people sunbathing on the grass verges whistled at the sight of Jake in his tight swim thin, but now it appeared he was amassing something of a junior fan club, determined to interrupt his training at every opportunity.

Sarah watched everything from high up on the raked seating, from where she could see the entire lido.

But watching Callum turned out to be impossible.

He didn't turn up.

When they had finished the session, Jake and Liam met Sarah outside the changing rooms.

'Any sign of him?' Jake asked.

Sarah shook her head. 'Nope, he definitely wasn't here.'

'And CJ said he didn't ring or leave a message to say he wasn't coming,' Liam added.

'Right,' said Jake. 'Let's go.'

'Go where?' asked Sarah.

'To Callum's house,' Jake replied. 'We need to ask him some questions.'

'What, like "do you have sap instead of blood"?' suggested Liam.

'I think we can be a bit more subtle than that,' said Jake.

Sarah glanced at her brother, still dressed in his fluorescent swim thin. 'You'd like to think so, wouldn't you? Why are you still wearing that thing?'

Liam ran his hands over his chest. 'Am I wearing it, though? Or is *it* wearing me on the inside?'

Jake blinked. 'What?'

'I'm trying to become one with my swim thin,' explained Liam. 'So that it feels like I'm swimming while wearing nothing at all . . .'

89

'Argh!' cried Sarah, rubbing her eyes with her fists. 'Don't say things like that! My brain is hurting just from trying not to picture it. I'll be joining Jake in the nightmare squad at this rate!'

They walked together in silence for a moment.

'Hang on,' said Liam, eventually. 'If the Creeper *is* posing as Callum, does that mean there are two of him now?'

Jake looked confused. 'What?'

'Think about it,' Liam continued. 'The Creeper can't take over other people's bodies—as far as we know—so that means he's just *disguised* as Callum. Well, according to you, anyway.'

'And?'

'And that means the *real* Callum must still be around somewhere.'

Jake's eyes widened. 'I didn't think of that.'

'Neither did I,' admitted Sarah. 'And I can't say I like the idea of there being two Callums to deal with.'

'So,' said Liam, 'If this *is* old plant-pants in disguise, what's he done with the *real* Callum?'

'We'll deal with that when we come to it,' said Jake, stopping outside a house halfway along the street. 'We're here.'

'Hang on,' said Liam. 'I thought you didn't like Callum?'

'I don't really,' said Jake.

'So, how do you know where he lives?' Liam suddenly looked hurt. 'Have you been round here playing *Brick-Quest* with him?'

Sarah turned away to hide her smile.

'Of course not!' Jake assured his friend. 'He got his school blazer mixed up with mine after PE once. My dad drove me down here so I could get it back.'

'Alright . . .' said Liam. 'I believe you.'

'OK,' said Jake. 'Ready?'

The twins nodded.

Taking a deep breath, Jake marched along the short garden path and rang the doorbell. After a moment, the door was opened by a short woman with greying hair.

'Yes, can I help you?'

'Hello,' said Jake as cheerfully as he could. 'We're here to see Callum.'

And that's when the woman burst into tears.

'He's in hospital?' asked Sarah, helping Callum's mum to settle back into her armchair. She passed her a tissue from a box on the side.

Mrs Ball nodded. 'In quarantine,' she sniffed. 'I'm only allowed to visit because I'm immediate family, and then I have to see him through a rubber curtain.'

'I would have thought that's the very best way to see—OW!' Liam was forced to stop talking when Jake stamped on his foot.

'How long has he been there?' Sarah asked.

'Just since yesterday,' Callum's mum explained. 'Since he got the moss on his skin.'

The trio glanced at each other.

'His skin has moss growing on it?' said Jake.

'The doctors think it's some sort of bug he picked up when we went on holiday to Brazil a few weeks ago,' said Mrs Ball. 'That's why they've put him in the tropical diseases unit.'

'When did Callum first notice this . . . moss?' asked Jake.

Callum's mum didn't reply. Instead, she jumped to her feet and tucked the tissue up the sleeve of her cardigan. 'Oh where are my manners?' she said with a smile. 'We've got visitors!' Then she hurried out of the room.

Liam sighed heavily. 'I hate to admit it, but I think Jake might be right this time.'

'Why?' asked Sarah.

Liam stared at his sister. 'Why? Because you don't

start growing moss on your skin—'

'—Or have a green tongue,' Jake reminded them.

'*Or* have a green tongue, if you're a normal human being. And trust me on this, I'm being very generous in describing someone like Callum Ball as a normal human being.'

'But, if he was the Creeper instead of the real Callum, why would he let his mum take him to hospital?' Sarah asked.

Liam opened his mouth to reply, then closed it again. He had no idea.

Mrs Ball bustled back into the room, carrying a tray with four glasses of green-tinged water sitting on it. 'I'm afraid I wasn't expecting company,' she said. 'So, I haven't got any squash in the house. It will have to be water ...'

She placed the tray down on the coffee table and took a glass for herself.

'Don't be shy,' she said. 'Help yourselves.'

'I'm good, thanks,' said Jake, wincing as he watched Callum's mum take a sip of the discoloured water. 'Are you sure that's safe to drink?'

'Oh yes,' said Mrs Ball, absent-mindedly pulling up the sleeve of her cardigan and scratching at her arm. 'The man from the water board was on TV this morning, saying that the funny colour is just a problem

93

caused by the drought. We've been drinking it and it tastes fine, so it must be OK.'

She scratched at her arm again.

'Right!' blurted Sarah, jumping up. 'We'd better be going. Don't want to be late for tea!'

Liam checked his watch. 'But tea isn't until—OW!'

This time it was his sister who had stepped on his foot.

'Why does everyone keep doing that?!'

Mrs Ball stood up and led the way back to the front door. 'Thank you for coming around to ask about Callum,' she said. 'I know you must have been very worried about him when he didn't come to swimming practice today.'

'Very worried,' said Jake with a smile.

'Perhaps you could come and visit him when he's back at home?' she suggested. 'He never seems to bring friends around these days.'

'There's a reason for that,' hissed Liam under his breath. He hopped out of the way before anyone could trample on his toes again.

'We'll pop round as soon as we can,' replied Sarah, ushering the boys out of the door.

'Goodbye!' called out Mrs Ball, waving to the children as they hurried back along the path.

They were several houses away before Sarah looked

back to check that Callum's mum wasn't watching them any longer. 'Did you both see that?' she said breathlessly.

'Yeah,' said Liam. 'I did. I mean, I'm sure his mum is fond of him, but who keeps a picture of her baby son in the bath on top of the TV?' He shuddered.

'Not that!' snapped Sarah. 'Didn't you notice Callum's mum scratching at her arm?'

'She's probably just got a mole or something,' said Liam. 'I've got one on my back, right between my shoulder blades. I call her Mole-issa!'

'Moles don't itch,' said Sarah.

Liam shrugged. 'OK, then—an insect bite.'

Sarah ignored him. 'It wasn't a mole or a bite,' she said. 'I could see her arm from where I was sitting. The bit she was scratching was green, and fluffy. Like moss!'

Jake blew out his cheeks. 'In that case, there's only one thing to do.'

'There is,' said Liam, frowning.

Jake nodded. 'We have to go and see Callum in hospital.'

'But his mum said only immediate family were allowed to visit patients in the tropical diseases unit,' said Sarah.

Jake forced a smile. 'Then I guess we'll have to break in.'

CHAPTER NINE

HOSPITAL

Twenty minutes later, Jake, Sarah, and Liam were sitting on the top deck of the number forty-two bus, as it wound its way through Larkspur town centre.

'When you said we were going to see Callum, I didn't think you meant right away,' said Liam. 'I'm not exactly dressed for a trip to the hospital.'

Jake looked his friend up and down. 'There's no location you're currently dressed for,' he commented. 'Unless we were heading somewhere to train as eco-ninjas.'

'Very funny!' said Liam, trying not to smile at the comment. 'I'm on a strict training diet at the moment, and I've got half a dozen raw eggs waiting for me in the fridge at home.'

'You're eating raw eggs?' said Sarah, pulling a face.

'Eggs are a good source of protein,' Liam retorted, 'and eating them raw ensures they keep all their natural nutrients and stuff. Tons of body builders eat them. I read it.'

'You read it?' said Jake. 'Where?'

'In a book, ages ago now . . .'

'You'll have to be a bit more specific than that if you want to convince me,' said Jake. 'Which book?'

'I dunno,' said Liam with a shrug. 'Just some book.'

'Come on, which book was it?'

Liam sighed, his cheeks reddening. 'One of the *Mr Men* books,' he admitted.

Jake and Sarah glanced at each other, and burst into laughter.

'*Mr Men*?' giggled Sarah.

'Mr Strong eats them every day before breakfast!' said Liam. 'He swears by them.'

'Oh well, so long as you've got the opinion of a professional . . .' mocked his sister.

Jake wiped tears from his eyes. 'Thank goodness you didn't pick up a copy of *Winnie the Pooh* by mistake. You'd be sticking your fist into a jar of honey right now!'

Despite his embarrassment, Liam grinned. 'It would taste better than the eggs.'

'It's probably just as well we're going to the hospital if that's what your diet is like at the moment,' said Sarah.

'That's the other thing I'm not sure about,' said Liam. 'There's some weird disease in town, and we're off to see someone who's got it!'

'Are you worried about catching it?' Jake asked.

'Of course!' replied Liam. 'I don't fancy spending the rest of the summer bright green!'

'Of course you don't,' said Sarah. 'You'd never know if you were wearing your new swimming suit or not.'

'Ha ha, very funny.'

'We can't wait,' said Jake. 'We have to find out how the Creeper is doing this.'

'*If* it's the Creeper doing this,' Sarah pointed out. 'I know you want this to be his fault, but it *could* just be a coincidence . . .'

'What? The water's turned green and manky, and it's putting people in hospital—it certainly sounds like the Creeper to me.'

'I'm not saying it's not him,' said Sarah. 'But it could just as easily be some horrible bug from Brazil, like the doctor thinks, or a problem the water company don't want to admit to.'

'Well, we're about to find out,' said Jake, ringing the bell as their stop appeared.

98

The trio hopped off the bus and crossed to the main entrance of the hospital. A pair of burly security guards checked them out as they passed through the vast revolving door and into the reception area.

Liam shivered as the artificially chilled air hit them. 'I wish I *had* got changed now,' he said. Then he spotted the racks of sweets, crisps, and sandwiches inside the entrance of the gift shop and his stomach gurgled. 'Food!'

'Off you go, then,' said Sarah. 'We'll wait here for you.'

Liam held out his hand. 'Can I borrow some money?'

'What? Where's yours?'

Liam ran his hands down the sleek material of his skin-tight swim thin. 'No pockets.'

Sarah pulled a handful of coins from her pocket and passed them over. 'You can pay me back later.'

'Of course!' said Liam. Then he was off, dodging through the crowds of hospital staff, visitors, and patients milling around. Among them, watching everyone closely, roamed three more large, uniformed guards.

He stopped at a rotating display of chocolate eggs in the shop entrance and began to turn it as he browsed the treats on offer.

'So,' said Sarah, turning back to Jake. He was studying a printed layout of the hospital on the wall. 'Where are the patients with tropical diseases?'

'No idea,' Jake admitted. 'The wards on here just have letters and numbers. It doesn't say what each of them is for.'

'We could ask at reception,' Sarah suggested.

Jake eyed the nearest of the security guards. 'We don't want to arouse suspicion. Callum's mum said only immediate family are allowed to visit, remember?'

Sarah smiled. 'Then that's who we'll say we are!'

Before Jake could stop her, she turned and marched towards the reception desk. He quickly caught up.

'Can I help you?' said the woman behind the counter, smiling.

'I hope so,' said Sarah, just as brightly. 'We're looking for the tropical diseases ward.'

The receptionist ran her finger down a laminated list taped to her desk. 'There are two wards that deal with those patients,' she said. 'Who are you here to see?'

'Callum Ball,' replied Jake, watching as the receptionist tapped the name into her computer.

'OK, he's registered as a patient,' she said, reading from the screen, 'But I'm afraid visiting is restricted to close relatives only. Next!'

The woman in line behind Jake and Sarah made to take a step forward, but the pair didn't move.

'I'm sorry,' said Jake, 'but we *really* need to know which ward Callum is in. It's very important.'

'And so are the hospital rules,' said the receptionist flatly. 'Only immediate family members are allowed to visit patients under the tropical disease team. Now, if you will be kind enough to step aside . . .'

The woman behind the pair tapped Jake on the shoulder and fixed him with an angry stare.

'Come on,' said Sarah, as the pair stepped aside, 'we won't get anywhere here . . .'

'If we just had some sort of distraction, I could probably get a peek at that computer,' said Jake.

Suddenly, there was a CRASH from behind them, accompanied by a number of shouts and screams. Liam had been spinning the chocolate display faster and faster—to the point where it had spun off its base, sending confectionery eggs of all flavours and sizes shooting out into the reception area.

Some of them hit people on the side of their heads, others skittered across the tiled floor where they became squidgy obstacles for visitors to slip and slide on.

At the first sounds of chaos, the receptionist abandoned her post and raced to help people up from the floor.

Jake shook his head, grinning at the sight of Liam as he tried to put the display stand back together. 'You can always rely on him to cause a scene!'

Sarah kept watch as he leaned over the receptionist's counter and checked the computer screen.

'Got it!' he said. 'He's in ward F2, on the seventh floor.'

'Good work!' said Sarah. 'Now, let's go and get the walking accident and head up there.'

By the time they reached Liam, he was cowering from the angry shouts of the shop's assistant—an elderly woman with blue rinsed hair and an amazing vocabulary of stinging insults and unpleasant threats, most of which involved the few remaining chocolate eggs.

'Everything OK?' Sarah asked her brother.

Liam shrugged. 'I've tried to explain it was an accident, but she won't listen!'

'Perhaps we'd better just leave,' suggested Jake.

'That's the best idea I've heard all day!' snapped the woman, pushing Liam until he was over the shop threshold. 'And don't come back!'

'Wow!' said Jake as the trio made their way towards the bank of lifts. 'She really wasn't keen on you, was she?'

'Not one bit,' said Liam. 'And you don't know the worst of it.'

'What's that?' asked Sarah.

Liam rubbed his hands over his stomach and sighed. 'I'm still hungry!'

DING!

'This is us,' said Jake, stepping out of the lift.

The seventh floor was deserted and, if anything, even chillier than the large reception area downstairs. It felt eerie, especially after the hustle and bustle of the ground floor.

'Ward F2 is down there,' said Jake, pointing along the corridor opposite the lift bank.

At the far end, the group could see the rotund figure and dark-blue uniform of yet another newly-hired security guard.

'Now we've just got to get past him,' said Sarah.

'That won't be easy,' said Jake, 'Because of that reporter bloke. What's-his-name . . .'

'Hacker Murphy,' Sarah reminded him.

'Yeah, him,' said Jake. 'Knowing him can be useful at times, but he's caused us a shedload of trouble by sneaking up here last night.'

'If it *was* him,' said Liam.

'Can you think of anyone else as obsessed with the Creeper as us?'

'Fair enough,' said Liam.

'*Doctor . . .*'

Liam peered down the corridor at the security guard again. 'We could tell him the truth,' he suggested. 'If the Creeper *has* caused the water problem, then he's as much in danger as anyone in Larkspur . . . He might listen.'

'I doubt it,' said Jake. 'Knowing our luck, he'll be a grown-up version of Callum himself; all brawn and no brains.'

'*Excuse me, doctor . . .*'

'And we've still got no evidence that the Creeper is anything to do with this,' Sarah reminded them. 'No matter how many people start sprouting moss on their skin.'

'But—' began Jake.

'No buts,' said Sarah, raising a hand. 'Until we've got proof, I'm keeping an open mind, and I suggest you both do the same.'

'Doctor, can you help me?'

A small, delicate hand landed on Liam's shoulder. The trio turned to find themselves faced with the radiant smile of a petite, elderly woman clad in a soft, pink dressing gown and slippers. The door to the second lift slid shut behind her.

'Doctor, do you think I could have a quick word?'

'I'm sorry,' said Liam, taking the woman's hand from his shoulder and squeezing it between his own. 'I'm not a doctor.'

'Well, of course you are!' said the woman with a frown. 'I'd recognize your beautiful green uniform anywhere!'

'No,' said Liam, 'I'm sorry. I'm not a . . . Do you think this shade of green suits me?'

The woman nodded, her face splitting into a wide grin. 'I most certainly do!' she said.

Liam looked at Jake and Sarah. 'Did you hear that, guys?' he asked, smugly.

Sarah shook her head slightly, unable to hide her smile.

Liam turned his attention back to his new friend. 'Now, how can I help you, Mrs . . .?'

'Well, it's Mrs Reid, but you can call me Eileen, dear,' said the woman. 'Everyone does!'

'Eileen it is,' said Liam. 'And you can call me . . .' He spotted Jake and Sarah vigorously shaking their heads out of the corner of his eye. 'And you can call me Doctor Ian Jection. These are my colleagues, Steph

O'Scope and Ivor Payne.'

Jake took a sidestep and stuck his tongue out at Liam over the woman's shoulder.

'My goodness!' gushed Eileen. 'Doctors seem to get younger and younger these days, don't they?'

'You don't know the half of it!' muttered Sarah.

'Now, how can we help you, Eileen?' Liam asked.

The patient's cheeks flushed a little. 'I'm rather embarrassed to admit that I'm lost,' she said. 'I left my ward to have a bit of a potter about and stretch the old legs, but I can't seem to find my way back.'

'Don't you worry,' said Liam. 'Now, which ward are you staying on?'

'D21,' Eileen replied.

'Right,' said Liam, resting a hand on the woman's shoulder and leading her forward slightly. 'Can you see that security guard at the end of the corridor down there?'

Eileen squinted. 'Yes, I see him . . .'

'Well, if you go down there and tell him which ward you're looking for, he will escort you back there, all safe and secure.'

'Just like that?'

'Just like that,' said Liam. 'It's all part of Extra Security Guard Day, which we're having at the hospital today.'

Eileen's face split into a wide smile. 'Is that what today is? I thought I saw lots of men in uniform when I popped down to the shop for my newspaper earlier. I always read the *Larkspur Chronicle*, you know . . .'

'So do I!'

Eileen shook Liam's hand warmly. 'Thank you, Doctor Jection!'

'Please, call me Liam . . .'

'Ian,' said Jake quickly.

'Call me Ian!'

'Well, I'm very pleased I bumped into you today, Ian!' said Eileen. With a wink back at the trio, she set off along the corridor towards the security guard.

They watched as she engaged him briefly in conversation during which Eileen shook her head several times. Then she took the big man's arm, and the pair set off through a set of double doors to their left, and disappeared.

'And the route to the tropical diseases unit is clear!' said Liam, taking a bow.

'That was brilliant!' grinned Jake. 'I take back everything I said about your hair, I don't care what colour it is.'

'I'm glad to hear it,' said Liam. 'It was nothing, but—hang on! What have you been saying about my hair?'

'Let's go,' said Jake, ignoring him. 'We don't know how long Eileen will distract that guard for.'

The group hurried towards the entrance of the tropical diseases unit, the rubber soles of their shoes squeaking on the polished hospital floor. Pushing open the doorway, they found themselves in an outer room where medical equipment and supplies filled shelving units around the walls. A large porcelain sink sat to one side. Sarah crossed to examine it, quickly gesturing for the boys to join her.

Jake and Liam hurried over. There were stains around the inside of the sink—like the tide mark left behind after a much-needed bath. But these stains were thick, gloopy, and green. Liam reached out towards the gunk, but his sister pulled his hand away before he could touch the gloop.

'We don't know what it is!' she hissed.

Liam shrugged. 'Looks like that stuff you get in ponds. What's it called? Algae! If it is, it should be harmless, shouldn't it?'

'It *should* be,' Sarah said, 'but with everything that's been going on, I wouldn't risk it.'

'Guys!' whispered Jake. 'Over here.'

Two sets of doors led off from this room—one to the right with darkened windows, and one straight ahead from where soft lighting glimmered. Jake led the way to the lit room. They gathered at one of the windows and peered through.

On the other side of the glass was a small room containing six beds, each one occupied by a patient and surrounded by a clear, plastic curtain. The curtains made it difficult to identify any of the individual occupants, although it was obvious that each of the patients had a range of medical machinery surrounding them.

'Which bed do you think is Callum's?' Liam whispered.

Sarah shrugged, but Jake didn't reply. His eyes were fixed on the furthest bed from the door. Liam squinted and followed his gaze.

Someone was inside the curtained area, moving around the bed and occasionally stooping to peer closely at its occupant. Liam swallowed hard. No, it wasn't someone—it was some*thing*.

It was difficult to see exactly thanks to the distorting effect of the thick, plastic curtain, but certain features were horrifyingly clear.

Over six feet tall, the creature was painfully thin, and had what appeared to be rough, brown skin— much like tree bark. Clumps of wild green hair sprouted from its scalp and its long, twisting arms ended in narrow, twig fingers.

'OK,' croaked Sarah, her mouth suddenly dry. 'It seems you were right all along ...'

Jake nodded numbly, getting no satisfaction at all from being proved correct. He forced himself to breathe, unable to tear his eyes away from the spectacle unfolding before them.

There, bending over one of the patients as though examining him, was the Creeper.

CHAPTER TEN

HIDE

Jake stared in horrified silence as the monster leaned deeper over the person in the furthest bed. It was all too easy to imagine one of them lying there instead, unable to move through fear.

Sarah clamped a hand over her mouth as the Creeper reached out and appeared to stroke the patient's cheek. She could imagine the sharp scratch as the creature dragged its twig finger across her skin.

Liam, however, gave up all pretence of staying quiet. He grabbed Jake's shoulder, shook it hard, and yelled, 'Look out! It's the Creeper!'

Inside the ward, the Creeper spun to stare at the doorway. Jake ducked beneath the window, pulling Sarah and Liam down with him.

'What did you do that for?' he demanded.

Liam shrugged. 'I couldn't help myself!' he replied. 'After listening to you blurt it out all summer, I guess it was just fresh in my mind.'

'Well, if we're in luck he won't have seen us, and we can get—'

'Shh!' hissed Sarah. 'Listen!'

CLICK! CLICK! CLICK! CLICK! CLICK! CLICK!

'He's coming this way!'

Jake slowly rose up and risked a glance through the window. It was true! The half-man, half-plant beast had come out from behind the transparent curtain, and was walking steadily towards the door.

CLICK! CLICK! CLICK! CLICK!

'Quick!' cried Jake. 'We have to hide!'

'This way!' said Sarah, turning and running for the nearest door. They crashed through, finding themselves in another ward almost identical to F2, but empty. The beds were stripped, their sheets and blankets stuffed into a large laundry skip on wheels at the far end of the room.

And there was no other way out.

CLICK! CLICK! CRRREAAAKK!

They heard the door to the other ward swing open.

Jake tried to ignore the pounding of his heart

thumping in his chest and crossed his fingers that the creature would head straight down the corridor.

CLICK! CLICK! CLICK! CLICK!

The sound of wood on tile grew louder. The Creeper was coming their way.

'Quick!' Jake whispered urgently. 'Hide!'

Sarah grabbed the handle of a cupboard and pulled open the door, revealing a line of identical chunky white suits—like astronaut's spacesuits—hanging on a rail. She squeezed in among them and quickly shut the door.

Jake and Liam dropped to the floor and slid under adjoining beds.

C-R-R-R-E-E-E-E-A-A-A-K-K-K!

The door to the disused ward opened achingly slowly.

Jake heard Liam take a deep breath and struggled to turn to him in the cramped space under the hospital bed. He pressed his finger to his lips, urging his friend to stay quiet.

Liam nodded. Jake could see that he was scared. He was trembling, and he had curled his hands up into fists, as though ready to come out fighting. Would that work? Could they take on the Creeper and win? Personally, Jake didn't want to find out.

C-R-R-R-E-E-A-A-K! CLICK! CLICK! CLICK!

114

The door swung closed, and the Creeper crossed the empty ward. Jake took a deep breath and tried to hold it. He had no idea how good the hearing of a half-plant monster might be, but he didn't want to give himself away.

CLICK! CLICK!

Two wooden feet, like the ends of twisted tree branches, appeared at the foot of the bed and stopped. Jake couldn't tear his eyes away from them. Each of the toes had leaves sprouting from them, and there were twisted knots in the bark where the ankles should be.

He glanced over at Liam. His friend had his eyes screwed closed, and he was mouthing something to himself—silently, over and over again.

Jake felt the sensation of panic wash over him. This was like one of his bad dreams, except in those he could at least run away from the Creeper. Plus, even in the midst of the very worst nightmare possible, he would always wake up and eventually realize he wasn't in any actual danger. But this was different.

Here, he was trapped. For real. All the freakish fiend had to do was bend down and look under the bed, and he'd be found.

He cursed himself for choosing such a ridiculous place to hide. Admittedly, he hadn't had much choice—especially with the lack of time—but he was now certain that he would be caught at any second.

And once the Creeper had caught him . . . Well, that didn't bear thinking about.

CLICK! CLICK! CLICK! CLICK!

The Creeper turned away from the beds, and crossed the room, heading for the cupboard where Sarah was hiding. Had she made a sound, given herself away? It was possible. All Jake could hear at the moment was his own blood pumping as it raced around his body.

CLICK! CLICK!

Jake slid forward to watch as the timber terror reached the cupboard and stretched a gnarled hand towards the handle. He saw something move out of the corner of his eye, and turned to discover that Liam was about to come out of hiding, presumably to protect his sister. But she hadn't been discovered yet! Liam could be giving himself away for nothing!

Jake waved furiously, hoping his friend would look his way before he made the mistake of revealing himself. Thankfully he did, and Jake was able to gesture for Liam to stay where he was.

'But, Sarah . . .' mouthed Liam.

'I know!' Jake mouthed back. 'We'll help if we need to, but not yet?'

Liam looked confused. 'Hell is a green poo, dropped by a yeti?' he mouthed.

Confused, Jake shook his head and turned his attention back to the opposite side of the ward.

The Creeper's long foresty fingers wrapped around the handle and slowly twisted it down. Both Jake and Liam watched in dread as the creature pulled at the door.

It didn't move.

The Creeper tried again, pulling harder this time. Still the door didn't open.

It was locked!

Jake breathed a sigh of relief. Sarah must have found a way to drop the catch from the inside. But his celebratory mood was short-lived. Extending a long finger, the Creeper pushed it into the gap between the door and the cupboard frame, sliding it up until the latch lifted.

THUNK!

The Creeper withdrew his finger, gripped the handle again, and pulled. Jake readied himself to scramble out of hiding and pounce—although he had no real idea what he could do to stop the monster.

The Creeper paused. Jake and Liam exchanged glances. Why hadn't it grabbed Sarah and dragged her out of her hiding spot? They both shuffled forward to find out.

The monster was busy searching among the dozen

or so suits hanging on the rail. It slid them first to one side, and then to the other. One of the suits fell from its hanger, landing in a heap on the floor of the cupboard.

Frustrated, the leafy lowlife reached further in and Jake could hear the sound of wood scraping against wood as their foe's hard hand tested the back of the cupboard to see if it was secure. But it found nothing.

Sarah wasn't in there.

The Creeper slammed the cupboard door closed and hissed with frustration.

Jake slumped down with a silent sigh, the tiles cold against his burning cheek. Wherever Sarah was, she was safe—for now. But he and Liam were still in danger.

CLICK! CLICK! CLICK! CLICK!

This was it. The Creeper had turned and was coming back their way.

The two boys locked eyes, hardly daring to breathe.

You idiot! Jake said to himself. *You're going to be caught for sure, this time!*

His eyes darted about, searching for a way to somehow hide even deeper.

CLICK! CLICK! CLICK! CLICK!

The footsteps came closer and closer, and then, as expected, the Creeper bent double, his burning green eyes sweeping the darkened space beneath the beds like a pair of glaring emerald searchlights. The monster's mouth twisted into a cruel grimace as he saw . . .

. . . absolutely nothing.

Liam and Jake weren't there.

Straightening again, the Creeper turned and made for the door that led back into the outer room.

CLICK! CLICK! CLICK!

As the Creeper reached the exit, there was an almost inaudible SQUEAK! from one of the wheels on the industrial-sized laundry basket.

The creature stopped and turned back into the room, head tilted to one side as he listened carefully. But there was no further sound to be heard. Grinding his wooden teeth together, he opened the door and left the abandoned ward.

CLICK! CLICK! CR-R-R-R-E-E-E-A-A-A-K-K-K! CLICK! CLICK!

Liam made to emerge from behind the laundry skip, but Jake grabbed his arm to stop him. He wouldn't put it past the Creeper to be out there still, watching through the windows in the doors, waiting for his victims to reveal themselves.

Having managed to slide along the floor beneath the beds and out to duck behind the metal trolley, they would have to remain still and silent a little while longer. But as a painful cramp begin to take hold of Jake's leg, he stood awkwardly and hobbled over to the doors, cautiously peering through the panes of glass.

Aside from a fresh batch of algae dripping over the side of the sink, the outer room was silent and empty.

The Creeper had gone. Jake didn't know where, but the fact that he wasn't within killing distance was enough for him at that moment.

Liam joined him, brushing dust from his swim thin.

'Any sign?'

Jake shook his head. 'Nothing,' said Jake. 'I hope he hasn't gone looking for more victims.'

'So long as the victims aren't us, that'll do me for now.'

'Where did Sarah go?' asked Jake, heading for the cupboard. He pulled open the door and the boys peered inside. As before, there was nothing but the row of thick, bulky suits and helmets to be seen.

Liam's eyes grew wide. 'You don't suppose there's a secret entrance to the kingdom of Narnia back there, do you?'

Suddenly, the suit that had fallen to the cupboard floor sat up and spoke. 'Don't be daft!'

Liam jumped, letting out a little SQUEAL!

Sarah clambered to her feet and stepped carefully through the door and into the ward, dressed in one of the suits. It was a white one-piece overall, with gloves and boots attached. A hooded helmet, complete with mesh visor, completed the ensemble.

'So, that's how you did it!' said Jake with a grin. 'I was certain he was going to find you.'

'So was I, even in the suit,' admitted Sarah. 'He actually touched my shoulder at one point. That's when I fell to the floor.'

'They look like those suits they wear in films when there's a radiation leak, or a deadly virus that no one can find the cure to,' said Liam.

'They are,' Jake confirmed. 'They're hazmat suits.'

'Hazmat?'

'*Hazardous materials*,' Jake explained. 'These things protect you from all sorts of stuff.'

'We could use them to inspect the patients next door without being infected,' said Sarah.

Jake grinned. 'That's brilliant!' he said, grabbing another of the suits from the rail.

It took nearly ten minutes for Jake and Liam to get into their own hazmat suits—mainly because Liam managed to put his on backwards the first time.

'Typical!' groaned Sarah. 'I got into my suit in the dark, silently, in a tiny cramped space.'

'Well, we can't all be as perfect as you,' scoffed her brother.

'Finally, you admit it!'

'I'm admitting nothing!' spat Liam. 'I know that I—'

'Enough!' interrupted Jake. 'Let's try to stay focused, OK? You can have your little sibling spat once all this is over.'

Liam huffed. 'Yeah, but she—'

'I said enough! These suits aren't exactly air-conditioned. I want to get in and out of the ward before I melt—or before the Creeper comes back looking for us.'

And so, trailed by a pair of grumpy twins, Jake led the way out of the disused ward and across the outer room to Ward F2. Another peek inside showed that there were still no staff around. Jake took a moment to try to steady his nerves, then pushed open the door and the trio slipped inside.

This ward was even hotter than the last. The air was stifling, and Jake wished he could lift up his headgear to wipe the sweat from his eyes—but he knew that would expose him to whatever diseases may be lurking in the air, so he resisted.

He set off in the direction of the corner bed and the patient the Creeper had been bending over, but stopped when he felt a tug on his sleeve.

'Look!' Liam exclaimed, pointing to the occupant of the bed nearest to the door. 'It's Arran Matthews, and he's unconscious!'

Jake pulled back the transparent curtain surrounding the cubicle to get a better view. Liam was right—it was Arran. And he was green. Not completely, but his skin had a green tint to it, and his hair was a dull emerald colour.

'Isn't that Jenni Cooke?' asked Sarah, moving to the next bed along where another unconscious patient lay. 'She was on your swimming team for a while, wasn't she?'

'And so was Mark Little,' said Liam, crossing to one of the beds against the far wall. 'In fact, I think everyone in here is someone that had to drop out of the Larkspur Lions because they fell ill.'

Jake turned to face the bed the Creeper had been so interested in. 'That means ...'

Together, the trio made their way to the far end of the room. Lying in the bed, covered from head to toe in thick, green moss, was Callum Ball.

Like the other patients, he was fast asleep. Unlike the others, he looked as though he was wearing an all-natural onesie and balaclava.

'I guess that's what you get for constantly drinking the polluted water,' said Jake.

'Athletes have to stay hydrated,' Liam pointed out.

'Yes,' agreed Sarah, 'But he looks like he's on the

verge of being pollinated!'

Jake reached out with his gloved hand and grabbed Callum's shoulder. 'Hey, Callum!' he said. 'Wake up, you've got visitors.'

But Callum didn't stir.

'Come on, lazybones!' said Jake, a little louder. 'Time to rise and shine.'

Callum remained asleep.

'This isn't good,' said Sarah. 'What do you think is wrong with them?'

'Frankly, we've no idea,' said a voice. The group turned to see who had spoken. There was now an extra figure in a hazmat suit standing right behind them.

The newcomer was taller than the children. Silently he ushered them out of the ward.

Once in the outer room Jake, Liam, and Sarah unzipped their hoods and removed them, glad to feel the cool air wash over them.

The recent arrival pulled off his own hood, revealing himself to be a middle-aged man with dark hair and a neatly trimmed beard.

'I'm Dr Benzine,' he said. 'I presume you three have come to visit your friends.'

Jake nodded. 'We're sorry,' he said. 'I know we're not supposed to be in there.'

'Oh don't worry about that,' said Dr Benzine. 'I've

never agreed with that ridiculous rule. If anything, I think it's good for these patients to have as many visitors as possible.

'Even if they don't know we're here?' asked Sarah.

'We can't be sure that's the case,' the doctor replied. 'Until we work out what's wrong with them, we don't know if they're aware of their surroundings or not.'

'Why won't they wake up?' asked Liam.

Dr Benzine shrugged. 'Your guess is as good as mine,' he admitted. 'In all my years treating tropical diseases, I've never seen anything like this.'

I'll bet you haven't, thought Jake to himself. *That's because you've never come across the Creeper before . . .*

Head made of twigs, dry grass, etc—resembles bird's nest

Hair = clumps of leaves/small bush (still not as stupid as Liam's!)

Piercing, green eyes

Wide mouth, crawling with insects

Sharp teeth. Brown. Broken sticks?

Arms too long to be human

Very thin body, like a narrow tree trunk

Fingers like twigs (Are they brittle? Can they snap?)

Long, spindly legs

Over six feet tall

Rough, brown skin. Bark?

How does the Creeper get from place to place without being seen?

Destroying the Creeper . . .

Can the Creeper be destroyed? What would I need to use?

Axe? (Check if Dad has one in the shed)

Fire? (Be careful it doesn't spread—dangerous)

Bury it? (Likely to just grow again)

Dutch Elm Disease (Possibly take too long)

CHAPTER ELEVEN

SPOKESMAN

That evening, Jake sat propped up in bed, his laptop in front of him, although he had grown bored of playing his favourite computer game, *Brick-Quest*, over an hour ago. Instead, he was doodling a picture of the Creeper using the paint tools, trying to work out where the freak's vulnerable areas might be—if it had any.

He paused to check the time. It was almost midnight, and he was tired, but he didn't want to settle down to sleep as he was certain that he would have another nightmare about the Creeper—especially after the day's unusual events.

He, Liam, and Sarah had climbed out of their hazmat suits and made their way back down to the hospital reception. The extra security guards were still on duty, but there was no sign that they had spotted anything wrong and, as staff and patients were milling about as normal, the trio figured the Creeper hadn't come down this far. Had he done so, there would almost certainly be an air of panic about the place.

Of course, that meant that the half-man, half-plant monster was still inside the hospital somewhere. Not an ideal situation by any means, but there was no way the three of them could search the entire building by themselves.

Jake briefly considered telling the whole story to one of the security guards, but remembered when he had tried to do the same at Larkspur police station. He hadn't been believed there, and there was nothing to say that the outcome would be any different here. Plus, he had spotted signs for the psychiatric unit, and he didn't fancy being checked in there as a patient.

So the three of them left the hospital, and caught the bus home. They sat quietly, each lost in their own thoughts about the day's events.

Now, several hours later, images of the Creeper's feet as they clicked over the tiles towards his hiding place were at the front of Jake's mind every time he closed his eyes. It was going to be a long night . . .

DDDRRRRRIIIINNNGGG!

Jake jumped as a new window suddenly appeared

on his laptop screen, and his headphones echoed with an electronic ringing sound. Who could be making a video call at this time of night? He clicked on the 'Answer call' button.

Liam's face appeared in the window.

'Hello, mate,' he said. 'Are you asleep?'

Jake blinked. 'Yes,' he said flatly. 'In fact, I'm sleep-chatting right now.'

'Well, you're luckier than me,' said Liam, missing the point entirely. 'I'm wide awake. Every time I turn the light off, I keep imagining the Creeper is standing in the corner of my room.'

'Welcome to my world,' said Jake with a sigh.

'So, what do we do next?' asked Liam.

'I don't think there's anything we can do,' Jake replied. 'Not unless we go back and search every ward in the—'

DDDRRRRRIIIINNNGGG!

A new window appeared next to Liam's, displaying an 'Add new caller?' button. Jake clicked it.

Sarah's face appeared. 'I can hear you talking through the wall, Liam,' she said. 'Are you chatting with Jake?'

Liam nodded. 'We're just trying to decide what to do next about the Creeper.'

'Although, I'm not sure there's anything we *can* do,'

Jake pointed out.

'That was my thought at first,' said Sarah. 'But then I went back to the beginning . . .'

'What do you mean?' asked Jake.

'Well, it all started with the water in the training pool, didn't it?' said Sarah. 'Whatever the Creeper did to it, it turned the water green.'

'And I've been swimming in it,' said Jake.

'Not as much as I have,' said Liam. 'I should be sprouting moss and lying in that hospital ward.'

'So, as much as I hate to admit it, you were probably right, Jake,' Sarah continued. 'The Creeper was most likely based at the lido and working from there.'

'I knew it,' said Jake. 'But now he's expanded and poisoned the water supply in the taps. He's going after everyone in Larkspur and the surrounding area. Perhaps even the entire county!'

'The hospital will need more than those extra beds in the tropical diseases side-ward,' commented Sarah. 'If this continues, thousands of people will get sick and start turning into plants.'

'And he's doing all that from the lido?' questioned Liam.

Sarah shook her head. 'That's my point. He'll have to be somewhere where he can get access to the main water supply.'

'The treatment plant,' said Jake. 'That old building a few streets away from school.'

'You think he's in there?' said Liam.

'It would make sense,' said Sarah.

Jake nodded. 'Then that's where we're going. First thing tomorrow.'

The next morning, the trio set off on their bikes for Larkspur's water treatment plant.

The building was an old Victorian design, towering high into the air, with wooden-framed windows and tall chimneys that seemed to reach for the cloudless sky above.

Jake tried one of the huge iron gates and found it unlocked. He swung it open. 'I guess they don't mind having visitors ...'

'Wait!' hissed Liam, 'We're just going in there?'

Jake shrugged. 'Why not?'

'Because, if we're right, the Creeper's in there. Right now.'

'And we're the only ones who can stop him,' Sarah reminded her brother.

'We're the only ones who *believe* in him,' Jake

corrected. 'Besides, if we find anything amiss we can tell the staff, and they should be able to put it right.'

Reluctantly, Liam lay his bike beside Jake and Sarah's, and the three of them walked along the path towards the vast main doors.

Unlike the gates, these were locked.

'So, what now?' asked Liam. 'Knock and ask if our unfriendly neighbourhood plant monster can come out to play?'

Jake ignored his friend's sarcastic tone. 'We'll find another way in.'

The trio walked around the building, and eventually found a side door that was ajar. They peered inside, but the lights were switched off and they couldn't see much in the darkness.

'What do you think?' asked Jake.

'I don't think we've got a choice,' replied Sarah.

'Oh, we have,' insisted Liam. 'We've got several choices. The one I like is going home and forgetting all about this.'

Sarah rounded on him. 'And what will we do when Mum and Dad are covered in moss and leaves, like everyone else in Larkspur?'

'We'll take it in turns to mow them,' said Liam with a shrug.

'You go home if you want to,' said Jake. 'I'm going

in.' And, with that, he stepped through the door and into the darkness beyond.

'Me too,' said Sarah, following.

Liam hesitated for a second, then scurried after them. 'I *know* I'm going to regret this . . .'

The atmosphere inside the water treatment plant was cold, and the three children found themselves shivering as their eyes slowly became used to the dim light.

They were in some kind of locker room. White coats hung in rows from pegs. Jake took one of them and pulled it on.

'Is that to make you look like you work here?' asked Liam.

'That, and to avoid my chattering teeth giving me away,' came the reply.

Sarah and Liam grabbed white coats of their own, and the trio left the locker room by the far door, continuing their exploration of the plant.

Further along the corridor, they found a large computer room, filled to the brim with equipment. The lights were bright and one wall was devoted to screens showing the circular tanks of water that sat in the land beyond the old, Victorian building. Each tank held hundreds, if not thousands, of gallons of water at different stages of the treatment process.

Liam made for the nearest computer terminal. 'I

wonder if this thing's got *Brick-Quest* installed?' he said. 'Imagine playing it on one of these massive screens!'

'Don't touch anything!' growled Sarah, slapping his hand away from the keyboard. 'You don't know what you're doing!'

'Actually, we have to touch it,' Jake pointed out. 'If we're going to save the people of Larkspur, we're going to have to disconnect the water supply.'

'You will do no such thing!' barked a voice.

The trio spun to find a man with greying hair and thin-framed, round glasses approaching from an office at the far end of the room. He was also wearing a white coat. 'Who are you?'

'My name is Jake Latchford,' said Jake in as friendly a tone as he could manage. 'These are my friends Liam and Sarah.'

'Hi!' said Liam, with a cheery wave.

'Can I ask who you are?' said Jake.

'I'm Melvyn Mulwray, Head of Public Relations for Larkspur Water Board,' replied the man.

'You're the person who's been on TV to say the drinking water is still safe,' said Sarah, recognizing the newcomer.

'That's right,' said Mr Mulwray, 'And that's because it is.'

'But, it's not!' countered Jake. 'The water supply has

been infected by a half-man, half—'

He stopped, realizing that the truth wasn't going to get them anywhere at all. Adults just weren't ready to believe in plant monsters.

'By an eco-warrior who calls himself the Creeper,' he continued. 'Whatever he's been putting in the water has already put half a dozen kids in hospital. If people keep drinking it, everyone will be poisoned! You have to shut off the supply!'

'Rubbish!' spat Mulwray. 'Larkspur's water has been through rigorous testing and all our experts agree that, despite a slight ongoing problem with discolouration, it is perfectly safe for human consumption.'

'That's because your experts don't know what to look for!' Sarah insisted. 'This isn't a natural bug, or even any sort of chemical that's been added to the supply. The Creeper has created a way to turn people into plants and infected the town's water with it.'

'Turn people into plants?' exclaimed Mulwray. 'Do you realize how ridiculous that sounds?'

'Yes,' said Jake. 'Yes, we do—but it doesn't stop it from being the truth!'

Mr Mulwray shook his head. 'Give me one good reason why I shouldn't call the police and have you children arrested for breaking and entering.'

'Because we don't want you to?' suggested Liam.

Mulwray ignored him and unclipped a walkie-talkie from the pocket of his white coat. 'Can I have security to the control room, please?'

'Please,' urged Jake. 'You have to believe us.'

'I have to do no such thing!' said Mulwray, as a tall, thin man with a shaven head entered the room. 'Ah, Stan . . . Would you please escort these three visitors off the premises?'

'Yes, boss!' said the security guard, offering up a half-hearted salute. 'Come on, you lot!'

'You're making a big mistake!' cried Jake as he, Liam, and Sarah were ushered from the room.

A few minutes later, the three of them were back out in the sunshine. The door to the locker room was slammed shut and securely locked.

'Well,' said Liam. 'That went about as well as we could have expected.' He turned to head back to the spot where they had left their bikes.

'Where are you going?' asked Jake.

'Home,' said Liam. 'We've got swimming practice in an hour.'

'We're not leaving,' said Jake. 'We've got to convince them to disconnect the water supply.'

'We tried, just now,' Liam reminded him. 'They said no.'

'And you're just going to accept that as an answer?'

asked Sarah.

'It doesn't matter whether I accept it or not,' said Liam. 'That *was* his answer!'

'And who do you think would give us an answer like that?' Jake demanded. 'Who, other than the Creeper himself?'

A look of surprise flashed across Liam's face. 'You think Mr Mulwray might be the Creeper?'

'It's possible,' said Jake. 'That could be why he's been going on and on about the water being safe to drink.'

'We can't rule out the possibility that he *is* the Creeper,' said Sarah.

Jake smiled to himself. All along, Sarah had been the first to roll her eyes and doubt that he had discovered the monster's secret identity. Now she was agreeing with him.

'And what if he's *not* the Creeper?' asked Liam.

'Then, we'll have to find a way to convince him that the Creeper is real, and that he's poisoning the water supply,' said Jake. 'And for that, we need evidence.'

Making sure they weren't being watched, Jake led his friends around to the back of the water treatment building. Ahead of them lay dozens of large, round tanks—each being stirred, swept, and filtered by rotating, mechanical arms.

'Have you noticed something about the water in those tanks?' asked Jake.

'It's not green,' said Sarah.

'Exactly!'

'So, that means it's all over?' said Liam.

'Unfortunately not,' said Jake. 'It just tells us that the Creeper is adding his secret ingredient—whatever that may be—somewhere inside there . . .' He pointed back at the old building.

Liam sighed. 'So, we're going back inside?'

'We're going back inside,' Jake confirmed.

'That could be easier said than done,' Sarah pointed out. 'The security guard locked the door, remember?'

Jake pointed to the windows in the rear wall of the treatment building. One of them was open slightly. 'Who said anything about doors?' He grinned.

They found a couple of old wooden pallets and stacked them up as a way to reach the window. It took a lot of lifting and pushing but, before long, the trio found themselves back inside the treatment plant.

The room they were in was almost completely dark; the grimy window they had just climbed through provided very little illumination.

'Careful!' warned Sarah. 'The floor's slippery. I think someone might have spilled something.'

Jake squinted. 'I can't see what it is.'

'Hang on,' said Liam. 'I think I can see a light switch over here . . .' He flicked it on, firing an ancient fluorescent tube-light into life.

Then all three of them froze.

The entire room—walls, floor, ceiling, and every inch of furniture—was covered with slimy, green algae.

'This is it!' hissed Jake. 'This is the stuff the Creeper is using to infect the water supply!'

'I think you're right,' said Sarah. 'Nobody touch it. We don't know how dangerous it is.'

'Then we were right,' said Liam, swallowing hard. 'The Creeper *must* be here . . .'

A cold, vicious cackle of laughter rang out.

CHAPTER TWELVE

TANK

Jake, Liam, and Sarah spun round—but there didn't appear to be anyone in the room with them. Suddenly the algae covering the far wall began to ripple and bulge. It stretched out towards them, then . . .

RRRIIIPP!

A long wooden arm punched out from beneath the vegetation. And another. Finally, with a sickening SQUELCH!, the rest of the Creeper tore through the green shroud and stood before them.

'Ssso . . .' he hissed. 'It appearsss you have found my sssecret lair!'

Jake shuddered. When the Creeper spoke, it sounded like someone snapping twigs and tearing bark from the trunk of a tree all at the same time.

He knew he wouldn't be able to forget the sound in a hurry.

'Not only have we found you,' said Sarah. 'But we know all about your plans to poison the water supply. And you won't get away with it!'

'Oh but I already have!' boasted the Creeper, stepping towards them. The usual *CLICK!-CLICK!* of his wooden feet was muted by the carpet of green foliage covering the floor. 'My initial victimsss are all ssstill in hossspital, ssslowly transsssforming into my children! Now the next ssstage of my plan isss ready to begin, I ssshall sssoon have the whole of Larkssspur under my control!'

The beast threw its wooden head back and laughed with a noise that reminded Jake of the burning logs on his grandparents' real fireplace. Another sound for his nightmare database.

'That's where you're wrong!' spat Liam. 'The kids in hospital are being kept away from the water supply, and it won't be long before the doctors have found a way to make them better.'

'And we're here to make sure you aren't able to infect the town's water supply any further,' Jake added. 'Admit it, fungus face—the game's up!'

The Creeper smiled, revealing sharp wooden teeth and a long, tree-root-like tongue that flicked around its bark-covered lips. 'The game isss never up!' bragged the monster. 'Although I admit it would have been easssier to take control of the population if the water I polluted didn't keep turning green . . .'

'Like the training pool at the lido,' said Liam. 'I may not have drunk any of your gross green goo, but I've been swimming in it all summer. But it didn't affect me—not like it did with Callum and the others. Why?'

The Creeper didn't reply but his glowing green eyes flicked up and he scowled.

Jake laughed. 'It's your hair!' he exclaimed. 'The bleach in your hair must repel the algae in the water! Think about it—the only kids left on the swimming team are those with bleached hair.'

Liam frowned. 'But, you didn't bleach your hair, and you've been in that pool.'

Jake's face fell as the realization hit home. Would he be next to grow moss on his skin and start to transform into one of the Creeper's "children"?

He had to get out and warn someone. Even the doubting Mr Mulwray would do at this point. If they could get him into the room to see the Creeper for himself, he would have to believe that they were telling the truth.

'Tell us about the algae!' he insisted.

'Really?' said Liam. 'You want freaky features here to keep talking?'

Jake nodded and gestured for his friends to follow his lead. Liam pulled a face, not seeming to understand, but Sarah did.

'Yes, we do!' she said firmly. 'We want every single detail!'

'It wasss easssy once I ssstarted!' the Creeper explained, seemingly eager for the opportunity to share his wicked plans with the world. 'I've alwaysss had the algae growing on my ssskin . . . mainly under my armpitsss . . .' He raised a painfully thin arm to reveal a clump of moist, green plant life clinging to the bark there.

Liam gulped. 'Wait! I've been swimming in your pit hair?!'

'It would appear ssso!' cackled the Creeper. 'And once I tear it out, it sssspreads ssso quickly!' To demonstrate, he reached up with his twig fingers and tore a lump of the damp algae away from his body. Then he tossed it against one of the few remaining bare spots on the wall and watched with glee as the greenery stuck, then took on a life of its own and began to spread outwards.

'I think I'm going to be sick!' said Liam.

'Go on,' Sarah urged the creature. 'We're

listening . . .'

'Once I realisssed I could ssspread my unique DNA by contaminating the water with this algae, it wasss jussst a matter of time before I made for the town ssswimming pool! You pathetic humansss brought thisss upon yourssselves, by gathering together in sssuch vassst numbersss!'

While the Creeper boasted about his plans, Jake slowly edged towards the far side of the room. If he could get to the window, he would be able to get out and call for help.

Liam finally worked out what his friend was doing and took a step towards the monster, staring deep into its emerald eyes and forcing the Creeper to stare back. 'Come on, then!' he urged. 'See if you can answer this . . . You were based at the lido the whole time, huh?'

'Of courssse!' hissed the Creeper, leaning in towards Liam, eyes unblinking. 'I had to disssguissse mysssself asss one of you mere mortalsss during the day while the place wasss open, but that wasss a price I wasss willing to pay in order to begin the creation of my own race of ssslavesss!'

Liam fought the urge to turn and run. Instead, he kept his staring contest with the Creeper going until Jake finally stepped out of the beast's eye line.

As soon as he'd achieved that, Jake grabbed an algae-covered metal chair, his fingers sinking deep into the coating of living, green matter. It made his stomach churn. He placed the chair beneath the window—the greenery on the floor masking the sound of the metal legs meeting concrete, and carefully climbed up towards the open window.

Sarah glanced behind the Creeper to where Jake was pulling himself up to the windowsill, then forced her attention back to the beast. 'Who were you?' she demanded. 'We thought we saw you just about everywhere.'

'Well, Jake did,' said Liam.

'Jake!' spat the Creeper, suddenly realizing that he was only talking to two children instead of three. 'Where isss he?!' The creature's eyes flashed a brighter green as they scoured the room.

Sarah groaned. 'Nice going, numb nuggets!' she barked to her brother.

Turning, the Creeper spotted Jake's trainers as his feet disappeared through the window. In a couple of bounds, the monster was up on the chair and clambering after him.

'We have to help him!' cried Liam.

'My thoughts, exactly!' said Sarah. She pulled her mobile phone from her pocket. 'No signal!'

'What are we going to do?'

'There's more than one way to use a mobile to call for help,' Sarah replied. Hurrying over to the doorway, she used her phone to smash the glass of the fire alarm. Instantly, a deafening bell rang out, causing Liam to clamp his hands over his ears.

'That'll probably do it!' he shouted. 'Now, let's get after Jake!'

By the time the Creeper landed beneath the window, Jake was almost at the first of the water treatment tanks. The monster quickly gave chase.

CLICK! CLICK! CLICK! CLICK! CLICK! CLICK!

Jake heard the sound of the creature's wooden feet clattering on the concrete and risked a glance over his shoulder. The Creeper was gaining on him, his long legs giving him the advantage.

Dodging between the water tanks, Jake ran as fast as he could. Images from his recent nightmares flashed through his mind—but this was no dream. This time the Creeper was chasing him for real, and who knew what the monster would do to him if he managed to catch up?

Jake fumbled in his pocket for his mobile phone, hoping he could call the police. There was an alarm ringing somewhere behind him, so the police would have to come and help—and this time, they would see the Creeper and believe such a thing existed.

He had dialled two of the three nines when the phone slipped from his grasp and clattered to the ground. Cursing, Jake skidded to a halt on the rough ground to turn back for it—and that's when the Creeper pounced.

Both Jake and the bark-covered beast tumbled over the side of the nearest treatment tank and splashed into the deep, dank water.

SPLASH!

Jake screamed as he plunged beneath the surface of the ice-cold water, a long stream of air bubbles escaping from his lungs and racing for the surface. He struggled to free himself from the Creeper's grip, but the solid branches of his attacker's arms were impossible to dislodge.

He gazed up at the sunlight flickering on the surface of the water above him. Sunlight that was rapidly fading. At first, Jake thought he was blacking out, but then he noticed a stream of thick, green goo pouring from the Creeper's armpits. The monster was filling the water with algae!

Within seconds, the sunlight had completely disappeared, and the only thing illuminating the water was the eerie glow of the Creeper's shining eyes.

Jake took his chance and poked his finger into one of the emerald orbs as hard as he could. The Creeper recoiled and released his grip enough for Jake to wiggle free and swim to the surface. He burst into the fresh air just as the tank's mechanical arm swept past.

'Jake!' came a shout from somewhere behind him.

Jake gulped down a lungful of air and turned. Wiping thick clumps of algae from his eyes, he saw Liam and Sarah racing in his direction. He opened his mouth to cry for help, but felt long twig fingers wrap around his ankle, and he was pulled under the water once again.

Liam and Sarah reached the edge of the tank and peered inside.

'I can't see a thing!' Liam cried. 'It's full of that horrible algae stuff!'

'Jake's under there somewhere!' said Sarah. 'You have to go in and get him!'

'Me?' exclaimed Liam. 'Why me?'

'One, you've spent all summer perfecting your swimming! And two, you have a built-in defence against the algae!'

'I do?'

Sarah grabbed a handful of her brother's bleached

hair and tugged. 'The bleach repels the stuff, remember!'

'OK,' said Liam, nervously, 'But the Creeper's in there ...'

A stream of air bubbles exploded on the surface, agitating the algae and causing it to multiply even further.

'And so is your best friend!' his sister yelled. 'But he won't be for long unless you save him!'

Liam stepped up on to the edge of the tank. 'I really wish I'd worn my swim thin today ...'

'GET IN THE WATER!'

Suddenly unsure whether he was in more danger in or out of the water, Liam dived in, narrowly avoiding a collision with the passing skimmer arm. It wasn't the best dive he'd ever executed, and the algae-thick water made more of a SPLUDGE! sound than a SPLASH! but, as soon as he ducked his head beneath the surface, the putrid pond plant scattered away from him.

Jake, still fighting to free himself from the Creeper, heard the noise and looked up. There was a sudden shaft of light where the algae had parted around Liam, but it disappeared just as quickly as his friend swam deeper.

Liam reached the bottom of the tank in a few strong strokes; all that training at the lido had paid off. He grabbed Jake's arm and pulled hard, but couldn't tug him free of the Creeper's clutches.

Jake breathed out a thin string of air bubbles, and Liam quickly realized that he had to act now, or his friend wasn't going to get out of the water tank alive.

He swung back his arm, and punched the Creeper in his foresty face, as hard as he could.

There was a CRACK! as the creature's head jerked back, and a bubbling GRUNT! of agony as Liam shook his hand in pain at what he was certain were now several broken fingers.

He'd just punched a tree!

Grabbing Jake with his uninjured hand, he kicked for the surface; the thick, oozing layers of algae parting as he swam harder than he had ever swum before.

The pair broke the surface to find Mr Mulwray and the plant's security guard glowering down at them. They didn't look very happy at all.

The two men reached down and hauled Liam and Jake out of the water, who both collapsed to the concrete, coughing and spluttering.

'Look what you've done!' bellowed Mulwray. 'These tanks aren't for playing in! It's dangerous to go in there!'

'You don't know the half of it,' gurgled Jake, spitting out a mouthful of algae. The stuff tasted like mouldy Brussel sprouts served in one of his dad's sweaty socks. Or so he imagined.

Mr Mulwray leaned over the edge of the tank and tried to part the green gunk on the surface with his hands.

'I wouldn't do that if I were you,' Sarah warned.

'Well, you're not me!' growled Mulwray. 'If you were, you'd know that Larkspur's water supply is now contaminated, and will have to be shut off until we can clean up whatever this stuff is your two pals have dumped in here!'

'That wasn't us!' protested Liam. 'That was the Creeper! And he's still in there somewhere!'

Mulwray ignored Liam and unclipped his walkie talkie. 'John, it's Melvyn,' he said into the handset. 'We need an urgent fresh water disconnection for the whole of Larkspur.'

'What, everywhere?' came the crackly reply.

'Everywhere,' Mulwray confirmed. 'And can you drain tank number four, please?'

After a few seconds, there was a THUNK! and the mechanical arm ceased its endless sweeping across the water's surface. Then the level began to drop.

Sarah helped the boys to their feet, and the trio steadied themselves, waiting for the Creeper to burst free of his watery hiding place.

But nothing happened. The tank drained completely, the water taking most of the algae with it.

Jake cautiously stepped closer to the edge and peered down. Aside from a thick ring of green gunge clinging to the sides, the tank was completely empty.

The Creeper had vanished. Again.

A siren rang out and a fire engine pulled up on the road outside the main building, closely followed by an ambulance.

'Go and tell them it's a false alarm, Stan,' Mulwray ordered the security guard. 'Although they might want to nip inside and check the backup filtration room. Someone has slopped some horrible green plant stuff all over the walls, ceiling, and floor. It might need testing to see if it's safe for us to clean up.'

The guard fixed Liam, Jake, and Sarah with a fierce stare. 'Did this lot do it?'

'I doubt it,' said Mulwray, shaking his head. 'It looks like it's been there for days.'

'That's a shame,' said Stan, looking genuinely disappointed that he couldn't blame the vandalism on the three kids.

'But,' added Mulwray with a wicked smile, 'We've got them for taking a dip in this here tank.'

Stan the security man cackled and rubbed his hands together.

'We didn't "take a dip",' Jake insisted. 'We chased your algae-spreading vandal to put a stop to him, and he pushed us in. There's no barrier or fence to stop anyone going over the side! You know, we are very friendly with a reporter at the Larkspur Chronicle . . .'

Mr Mulwray's cheeks paled a little. 'Yes, well . . . let that be a warning to the three of you.' he said. 'Water treatment plants are not swimming pools! Now, get out of here before I change my mind.'

Trying to hide their smiles, Jake, Liam, and Sarah turned and made for the gates that led out of the water treatment works.

'After all that, we still didn't get the Creeper,' said Jake with a sigh.

'He just seemed to disappear, like he'd gone down the drain,' said Sarah.

Liam nodded. 'He was definitely in that tank with us.'

A high-pitched giggle rang out, and the trio looked up to see the boy with ginger hair who had targeted Jake at the lido. The boy waved to them, then wiped his hand across his shirt, leaving behind a thick smear of bright, green algae. Laughing again, he skipped away.

Jake ran to the gates, Liam and Sarah at his heels. But, by the time he got out on to the street, the boy was nowhere to be seen.

Sarah stared, open-mouthed. 'You don't think that was . . .'

Jake shrugged. 'If it was, we've just lost him again.'

'Yes, but we saved you,' Sarah pointed out.

'We?!' cried Liam. 'I think that bit was down to me! And I picked up an injury in the process.' He held up his hand—two of his fingers were twisted and swollen.

'That looks nasty,' said Jake. 'But I'm very grateful.'

'You can prove it by taking me to that ambulance crew up there and then sitting with me in Accident and Emergency,' said Liam. 'I think my days of competing with the Larkspur Lions are numbered.'

'Still,' said Sarah as they set off towards the ambulance. 'We did succeed in getting the water supply disconnected until they've cleaned and disinfected everything, so there shouldn't be any more cases of plant poisoning.'

'That's true,' said Jake. 'With any luck, the side effects will begin to wear off now—especially for anyone who's been drinking the water *and* swimming in it. They're likely to be the worst hit.'

'Great!' groaned Liam. 'Callum Ball, back to full strength. Just what we need!'

'Oh, don't be so grumpy!' said Sarah, digging her brother in the side with her elbow. 'We have just saved the whole town—again!'

'Yeah, we have, haven't we?' said Jake with a grin. 'In which case, I'd say that today has gone swimmingly!'

CHAPTER THIRTEEN

HACKER

So there you have it. The latest case file in my investigations into the creature known as the Creeper.

Once again, it seems to be the same three children who were attacked by the monster; I managed to grab an interview with them when my editor sent me to cover the emergency measures taken at the water treatment works.

This time, they told me, the Creeper had been planning to infect everyone in Larkspur with his own DNA.

Thank goodness he didn't succeed in doing that. What would have happened if he had managed to turn everyone in town into a moss-covered clone of himself? It doesn't bear thinking about. The Creeper would have

159

an algae-powered army ready to spread out across the country, turning this green and pleasant land into, well . . . a green and rather unpleasant land.

You'll be happy to learn that the children in the tropical diseases ward made a complete recovery, although their parents have all commented that their normal childhood aversion to vegetables at mealtimes has developed into something much stronger.

Liam did indeed suffer two broken fingers as a result of his underwater encounter with the Creeper, which he had to have strapped together to enable him to continue swimming for the rest of the summer.

At the end of the season, Liam was awarded with the Swimmer of the Year award—which he dropped and broke as he was coming off the stage.

Jake didn't make it into the first team of the Lions that season, but I don't think he minded. He was just happy that Mr Mulwray of the water board didn't want to press any charges for the boys contaminating the water supply.

He did have to write a report as to what had happened for the water board's records, though—but Mr Mulwray didn't keep it once he'd read it. He said it was "some made-up nonsense about a stick man coming to life and chasing them around the plant".

I don't think I'll bother interviewing him for my

case files.

One person I *have* interviewed again and again now is Mr Roberts, the porter at the hospital. Since he helped me sneak up to the tropical diseases ward, he's called me several times a week, certain that he's uncovered another story for me. He's rung to tell me about everything from an infestation of fairies to Elvis Presley still being alive and admitted to the hospital with a slipped disc.

In fact, I'm just about to head back up to the hospital now. Roberts called me this morning, convinced that one of the nurses has been abducted by aliens.

Just another day in the life of an intrepid local newspaper reporter!

Stay safe, and don't drink green water . . .

Your friend,
Hacker Murphy

ARE YOU BRAVE ENOUGH
TO HANDLE MORE

CReePeR FiLeS?

READ ON FOR A TASTE OF

INCY WINCY EEK

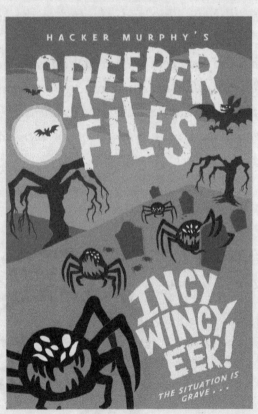

AVAILABLE NOW.

As Jake stood up, something brushed against his head. He jumped back, startled, then stopped when he realized it wasn't a Creeper-controlled plant vine or a ghost. It was a long strand of spider silk, hanging down from a high branch. It was several times thicker than any web he'd ever seen and must've taken the spider hours to spin. It almost looked like a thick piece of string made from hundreds of thinner strands, all twisted together.

'Cool, what's that?' said Liam. He took hold of the line and tugged sharply. The branch above them bent, but the web didn't break. Liam wrapped the web around his hands, then jumped and raised his knees to his chest. 'Check it out, I'm Spider-Man!'

'I'm not sure you should be doing that,' said Jake. It wasn't the web he was worried about, so much as the tree it was attached to. The afternoon was getting on, and the October shadows were making the tree look strangely sinister and threatening.

And not just that tree, either. The whole forest seemed to be squeezing in around them, long spindly branches reaching towards them like twisting claws and withered arms.

Liam stopped swinging and released his grip. Or he tried to. The web was stuck to his hands. He hooked an arm over it to try to give himself leverage, but the webbing stuck to his arm, too.

'Well, this is annoying,' he muttered, turning to try to untangle himself. Instead, it had completely the opposite effect. The web line snared around him, pinning the top part of his arms to his side. His hands were tied together in front of him.

'Want some help?' Jake asked.

'With what?'

Jake gestured to the tangle of webbing around him. 'Well, that.'

'Hmm? Oh, no. I've got this,' Liam said. He managed to bring his hands up and his head down enough to bite into the thread. His teeth immediately stuck to it, and he realized he was completely trapped.

'Well, 'is is awkward,' he managed to slur through his web-jammed mouth. 'Maybe 'ome 'elp 'ould 'e 'ood.'

'OK, wait there,' said Jake. Liam shot him a sarcastic look. It wasn't as if he could go anywhere. 'I need to find something to cut through the web.'

'What's happening?' Sarah called from the other side of the wall of spider silk. 'Have you found anything?'

'Er, no,' Jake lied. He knew if he told Sarah there was a giant spider's web, and Liam was trapped in it, she'd completely freak out. His eyes fell on something shiny and metallic propped up against the trunk of a tree. It was the gardener's shears. They'd be perfect for cutting through the web.

After quickly looking around to make sure their owner wasn't nearby, Jake grabbed the shears and very carefully snipped Liam free. Even with the sharp blades of the shears, it took all his strength to slice through the silk.

'I'm free!' Liam cheered, as Jake cut through a piece of the web. Liam's arm flopped loose, then immediately got tangled in another strand. 'Oh, no, spoke too soon.'

Jake lined up the shears again. He was just preparing to snip when a rustling from deeper in the woods caught his attention. He froze, peering back into the shadows.

'What is it?' Liam asked.

'Shh,' Jake whispered. 'I think I heard something.'

Liam swallowed. 'Was it something nice?'

The sound came again—a frantic rustle of something scrabbling through the undergrowth. Or maybe the undergrowth itself coming alive!

Jake looked at the tangle of web around Liam. He looked back towards where the rustling sound was starting to draw closer.

'OK, Plan B!' he announced, stretching up and slicing the thread above Liam's head. Liam was still tied up, but at least he could run. 'Let's get out of here!' Jake yelped.

Sarah stumbled backwards as the boys launched themselves through the web wall. It made a loud ripping sound as they tumbled through, but then they were back on their feet and, for the second time that day, running through the cemetery towards the gate.

'Come on, Max!' Jake hollered.

Max trotted out from behind the bush, his tail wagging. He loved chasing games, and Jake looked as if he was really putting effort into this one.

The little dog was about to give chase when he stopped and sniffed the air. His tail stopped wagging. He turned and glared into the forest, then growled way down at the back of his throat. The undergrowth rustled again, and Max decided his single growl was quite brave enough for one day, thank you very much. With a soft whine, he set off after Jake as fast as his legs would carry him.

Ready for more great stories?
Try one of these...

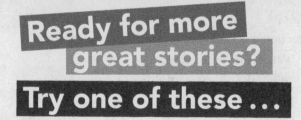